Second Chance Hawaiian Honeymoon

Cara Colter

HARLEQUIN
Romance

HARLEQUIN®

Romance™

Recycling programs
for this product may
not exist in your area.

ISBN-13: 978-1-335-73714-4

Second Chance Hawaiian Honeymoon

Harlequin Enterprises ULC
22 Adelaide St. West, 41st Floor
Toronto, Ontario M5H 4E3, Canada
www.Harlequin.com

Printed in U.S.A.

Cara Colter shares her home in beautiful British Columbia, Canada, with her husband of more than thirty years, an ancient, crabby cat and several horses. She has three grown children and two grandsons.

Books by Cara Colter

Harlequin Romance

Cinderellas in the Palace

His Convenient Royal Bride
One Night with Her Brooding Bodyguard

Matchmaker and the Manhattan Millionaire
His Cinderella Next Door
The Wedding Planner's Christmas Wish
Snowbound with the Prince
Bahamas Escape with the Best Man
Snowed In with the Billionaire

Visit the Author Profile page
at Harlequin.com for more titles.

Mahalo to my Hawaiian *ohana*,
the Woodwards and the Carters.

Praise for
Cara Colter

"Ms. Colter's writing style is one you will want
to continue to read. Her descriptions place you
there.... This story does have a HEA but leaves you
wanting more."

—*Harlequin Junkie* on *His Convenient Royal Bride*

CHAPTER ONE

BLOSSOM DUPONT made her way through the late spring crowds in the historic Gastown area of Vancouver. It was just one of those perfect days: the sun out; the leaves on the trees unfurling, fresh and green; something vibrant in the air.

Spring did this, didn't it? Made the whole world light up with a kind of hopeful energy.

She was not unaware of eyes on her, as she walked to her destination. She could feel a shimmer, deep in her belly. She wondered if it was that same aura of expectation that was in the warm spring day.

But somehow she doubted that it was anticipation and happiness shimmering in her.

It was that darned anxiety that she was trying so hard not to acknowledge.

Life's too good. The other shoe is going to drop.

Of course, that disturbing encounter with Joe's father hadn't helped.

Stop it, she ordered herself. Just stop it.

In a little over two weeks, she was going to

be married! She was well aware being loved had given her this newfound sense of coming into herself, so much so that most days she could ignore that little voice saying *Don't get your hopes up.*

Blossom didn't consider herself beautiful—though oddly she considered her identical twin sister, Bliss, exactly that.

And maybe Bliss, living up to her name, was beautiful because she had always radiated exactly the kind of energy Blossom was brand-new to.

Well, that and Bliss was way better with makeup, and hair, and clothes. Blossom liked as little fuss as possible. Before she'd begun dating Joseph Blackwell, makeup was a time-consuming nuisance. She rarely curled her long, dark brown hair or put it up. She'd had an absolute aversion to dressing up ever since her senior high school prom.

But as soon as Joe had asked her out, Bliss had placed herself in charge of the management of all things Blossom. Really? She should have appreciated having a private consultant making her look her best every day. The man was a billionaire! As Bliss had pointed out, you didn't go on a date with a man like that in wrinkled khakis and with a sunburned nose.

Blossom did appreciate her sister's efforts. Of course she did!

How convenient was it to have your identical twin sister's rather extensive wardrobe open to you? How wonderful was it to have your fashion-savvy sibling putting together outfits for you?

Right now, Blossom was wearing a short, black, flirty pleated skirt that swished around her thighs, slender boots with a skinny heel that added two inches to her height, and a filmy, pink pastel blouse, the lacy red camisole underneath just peeking through.

Bliss had pronounced, with satisfaction, that the outfit was sexy as hell and then she'd gone to work to make the rest of Blossom match. So, her abundance of hair was held loosely up in a clip, giving her a casual I-don't-care-what-my-hair-looks-like look that was devilishly hard to achieve. The dark suede brown of her eyes had been accentuated with artfully placed smudges of shadow. Her cheekbones looked high and her cheeks looked hollow. Bliss had declared Blossom's faintly glossed lips *kissable*.

"Who needs to have kissable lips to go out for lunch?" Blossom had asked.

"Lunch with Joe Blackwell," Bliss had reminded her.

Unfortunately, that reminder, and the faintly incredulous note in her sister's tone, brought out the very voice Blossom was trying to silence.

The voice that was asking her if Joe had fallen for *her* or for Bliss's creation. Because she'd been down this road before, hadn't she? Pretending to be something she was not. With catastrophic results.

Bliss's creation was attracting quite a bit of attention. It was a bit of a marvel, because, with one notable exception in her past, Blossom had never really been the woman who garnered male attention, and yet she could feel eyes following her with interest. A construction worker, uncaring of political correctness, bless his heart, wolf-whistled his appreciation.

She stopped in front of Essence, the new *it* restaurant in Vancouver. The restaurant did not take reservations, and hopefuls were lined up to the corner and beyond.

But those hopefuls weren't engaged to Joseph Blackwell. When he'd suggested lunch here, Blossom had said she didn't have time to wait in the line. Truth be told, she barely had time for lunch.

She had a wedding to get ready for.

A wedding in the final countdown. Sixteen days.

Of course, that was her job. She always had a wedding to get ready for. She and Bliss had started their wedding planning company, Blossoms and Bliss, three years ago. They liked to joke that their weird names, bestowed on them by their wildly eccentric artist mother, had finally paid off.

The company had taken all their money, all their heart, and every ounce of their courage. Several times they had thought it was over, that they were going to go under, that the dream was dead.

But then they had been hired by Vancouver real estate phenom, Harold Lee, to do his daughter's wedding. The Cinderella-themed, over-the-top wedding had moved their company into the awareness of people in entirely different circles. They were now fielding requests from dream clientele.

And, of course, it was because of the Lee wedding that Blossom had been introduced to Joe Blackwell, the groom's best friend and best man.

Nobody could have been more surprised than her when, at the end of the evening, he had asked for her—not Bliss, who was usually the one who was swarmed with the attention of any available male who had attended the wedding—if she would like to dance.

Normally, she would have said no. Normally, she would have considered it unprofessional.

And yet that night, the last dance of the night had been to the song "Hunger." The waltz, with its haunting melody, was about passion. Longing. And, finally, fulfillment.

And when Joe Blackwell had held out his hand to her, she had taken it, unable to resist. Since that first electrical touch, Blossom had known exactly what hunger, on every level, meant.

Now, all these months later, she was still unable to resist him, still hungry for his touch, his gaze, his slow, sexy smile.

After a whirlwind romance, she was about to marry a man who had actually laughed when she mentioned the line-up at Essence. He and the owner were old college buddies. There wouldn't be any line for them.

Of course there wouldn't, because Joe lived in *that* world.

And now, she thought with a tiny shiver, so did she.

But again, that shiver was nebulous. It could equally be happiness or bad nerves because Joe so obviously belonged in a world that she was still finding her way in, like a tourist lost in the mazelike streets of Paris.

Again, she remembered that stunning encounter with his father, James. The Blackwells were a well-known and well-heeled Vancouver family, what people often called *old money*. That evening, not even a week ago, Blossom and Joe had been invited for dinner at the Blackwell senior's estate in the tony British Properties in West Vancouver.

Joe's parents, James and Celia, had always *seemed* to like her.

And yet James had been standing outside of the bathroom door when she had come out, as if he'd been waiting for her.

I know what you're up to.

She had been stunned, but when she had pressed James for clarity, he had given her a dark look, gone in the bathroom and shut the door in her face.

Blossom shook it off as she stepped past the first people in line, ignoring their annoyed looks as she went out of the brightness of the day into the restaurant.

The woman at the front hostess station was one of those intimidating types. She was regal, all in black, with a string of tasteful pearls at her neck. She looked more like a member of an exclusive country club than a hostess at a restaurant, even a posh one.

She raised a perfectly shaped eyebrow at Blossom, asking, without saying a single word, who did she think she was? Hadn't she seen the line-up outside?

At least Blossom was finally able to identify the shiver within her. Nope. Not happiness. That voice.

"Not good enough."

"Imposter."

"Hopelessly out of her depth."

Joe's father's words had brought each of those insecurities she'd thought long buried rushing to the surface.

Without warning, she was once again the girl at the senior high school prom, the one who had the date with the star of the high school football team, whose mother had been so excited to find a Jacob Minstrel original gown at the secondhand store.

For once, Blossom had been the fairy-tale princess.

Until it had all fallen apart. She shivered. She did not want to think of that now. But because she had allowed it to creep into her thoughts, she had a sudden fear that maybe Joe—who had never stood her up or let her down—wasn't here, that this, too, was going to all fall apart.

She could almost hear her mother, always quick with the New Age advice—and also, ironically, the source of that fear that you could always count on things to go sideways—saying, *Fear is like saying a prayer for what you don't want.*

She took a deep breath and shook off the feelings. Instead of trying to tug the skirt down to cover an extra inch of her thigh, Blossom raised her eyebrow back at the hostess. "I'm Blossom DuPont."

There was that subtle sneer at her name—as if it was a stripper name—just the faintest lifting of a red-painted lip.

"I'm meeting Joseph Blackwell." She could not resist adding, "My fiancé."

The sneer disappeared as if the woman had tried to swallow her lips. Before her expression smoothed over completely, Blossom caught a flicker of envy, that look that said, *Why you?*

A question she had asked herself a hundred—

no, a thousand—times over the last action-packed months of romance.

"I'll show you—"

"It's okay, thanks, I see him," Blossom said, moving past the woman. She paused before she went into the main area of the restaurant. She understood that woman's envy completely.

When she saw Joe, she always had this sensation.

Pinch me. I must be dreaming.

Today, it was even more intense, a sensation of wanting, accompanied by a delicious flutter in her heart. In sixteen days, *this* sophisticated, handsome billionaire was going to be her husband.

Blossom admired Joe even more because he had not been satisfied to rest on his family's laurels. He had cut his own swathe to fortune with hard work and savvy, creating one of the most well-known software design companies in the world.

He wore his success with the confident ease of a man who had never expected anything less of his life than the lofty place he had arrived at. Whereas Blossom had to *work* at looking a certain way, elegance and good taste came to Joe as naturally as breathing.

Today, he had on jeans and a deep gray suit jacket, a crisp white linen shirt, undone at the throat. Even without a hint of a label showing anywhere, the cut and quality of that clothing screamed the expense and classiness of the very best men's designers in the world. He could leave lunch and be on for the cover of *Trends*, the men's lifestyle magazine that always had a hot, hot model on the cover.

Joe had all those cover-ready qualities: absolutely masculine, stunningly gorgeous, radiating masculine self-assurance.

The subtle restaurant light was playing with his perfectly cut light brown hair, spinning strands of gold into it. The soft glow showed his features to advantage, the beautiful nose, sculpted cheekbones, the faintest cleft to that strong chin, all of it with just a hint of whisker shadowing.

He had been studying the menu, but as if he sensed himself being watched, he suddenly glanced up. A smile touched his full, sensual lips, and revealed straight, even, beautifully white teeth. Blossom felt that familiar melting sensation.

Her fiancé. In sixteen days, she would be Mrs. Blackwell.

She savored the impact of those eyes that were taking her in with grave male appreciation. Joe's eyes were a shade of green deeper than the most valuable jade, and like valuable jade, seemed to spark from within.

She was pretty sure that was what she had loved about him first, how the light in his eyes deepened whenever he looked at her. Suddenly, Blossom was nothing but grateful for the outfit Bliss had selected.

Joe rose from the table as she arrived, took her shoulders and kissed her on both cheeks.

"You look gorgeous," he said, his voice so deep, so familiar, so sensual. His eyes lingered on those *kissable* lips.

And then he gave in and kissed them, the kiss lingering.

Blossom turned to liquid, hot and melting. He broke the kiss, but reluctantly, and she slid into the chair he held out for her, boneless.

"Sorry," he said. "I can't resist you."

There was just a tiny smudge of her gloss on his lips that she wanted to remove. Those green eyes sparked with something so hot, she considered suggesting they skip lunch.

Which, of course, would be *trashy*, a word that had haunted Blossom for nearly five years.

"Thank you," she managed to stammer. "You're looking pretty irresistible yourself. The hostess has the hots for you."

The hostess, me, any female breathing within a hundred yards or so...

He glanced over at the hostess station, lifted a shoulder, dismissing the compliment, looking back at her as if she was the only woman in his world worthy of note.

Something in Blossom sighed. He was so *perfect*.

"So, how's your day been?" he asked. His hand closed over hers and squeezed, and she squeezed back, marveling at the small intimacies that love imbued with the light of the spectacular.

"Busy!"

"You said today was busy, so I've been studying the menu trying to decide what you might like. I guessed the pear and brie croissant. What do you think?"

In what world was one of Vancouver's richest men trying to decipher what she might like for lunch? *Her world.*

But there was that cloud again. Pressing at her world of sunshine and blue sky, telling her, *Watch out. There's a storm brewing.*

"That sounds perfect," she said, hoping her tone was bright and chipper and not faintly uneasy. "Just like you."

He smiled at her, but, always hyperalert, Blossom thought she noticed something in his smile. Was he tired? So was she. Exhausted. But it would all be worth it soon.

"Can you believe we're in the final stretch? Sixteen days," she said to Joe, brightly. Again, she could feel something forced in her deliberately cheery tone.

He lifted his water glass to her. "I can't wait," he said.

Some intuition insisted on tickling along her spine. It felt as if he had left the sentence unfinished. As if what he wanted to say was, *I can't wait for it to be over.*

Well, she did this for a living. She knew, at this stage, everyone—but particularly the groom, it seemed—was exhausted with the inevitable minutiae of a wedding, especially an extravagant one.

"Just think, in seventeen days," he said, "we'll be on the Big Island."

Blossom had learned the island they were flying to—on Joe's company's private jet—the day after their wedding, actually bore the name Hawaii, but it was called the Big Island to distinguish it from the chain of islands that made up the State of Hawaii.

"Mr. and Mrs. Blackwell," Joe said. "On our honeymoon."

Again, there was a wistful, almost weary note, as if he would like to just skip over the whole wedding and get to the good part.

Not that the honeymoon wasn't going to be a good part—the Blackwells had friends who had turned over their entire Hawaiian estate for the enjoyment of the newlyweds—but Blossom had to stay focused on the tasks right in front of her.

For her, right now, the *good* part was the wedding, everything under control, a plan being skillfully executed, so that she and Joe and their guests could enjoy an absolutely amazing day.

"Speaking of the wedding," she said, though technically they had been speaking about the honeymoon, "I think we need to make a change to the menu. We should tweak dessert."

She had hung her bag over the back of the chair and twisted to get in the main pocket for the menu. "Here it is. I just scratched out the first choice and wrote in the other. I caught it before they were printed, thank goodness, and before the caterer carved it in stone."

She slid the sample menu across the table.

He took it and glanced at it, set it down and rubbed a hand over his face. He *was* tired. But her intuition was nagging at her. It was something more. Her hinky sense went on high alert. There was that shimmer.

Becoming uncomfortably electrical, and not in the good way, like when Joe claimed her lips with his own.

"Is everything okay?" she asked him.

"Sure."

But there was something in his tone that didn't sound *sure*.

"Is something wrong with the menu?"

He glanced at it again.

"I guess I was just wondering," he said, after a moment, "what a different kind of wedding would have looked like."

Blossom felt everything in her freeze, as if she had stopped breathing and turned to stone. As she looked across the table at her fiancé, she felt her intuitive sense crow, *Aha! This is the moment you've been waiting for.*

Bracing herself for, really, with her senior prom

disaster history, and even more so since Joe's father had said those words.

Ever so carefully, she unfroze herself. She forced herself to take a sip of her water. Ever so carefully, she said, "Sixteen days out, and you're wondering what a different kind of wedding would have looked like?"

Inwardly, she wondered how far that was from Joe wondering what a different kind of bride would have looked like.

Joe lifted a broad shoulder, clearly uncomfortable. He met her eyes, and then looked away. "Forget I said it."

As if that wasn't impossible!

"But what exactly does that mean? A different kind of wedding?" she asked, unable to let it go. Despite trying to strip the note of hysteria from her voice, she could hear the brittleness in her tone.

This is what she *did*.

Weddings. Perfect weddings.

And hers was going to be the most perfect of them all. Everything was in place. A venue to die for. The best catering in Vancouver. A live band to dance the night away to. The most incredible wedding gown ever…she was going to be a princess. And this time, no clock was going to go off at midnight to return her to the scullery.

"What does that mean?" she asked, again, when Joe didn't answer right away.

He met her gaze. This time he didn't look away. "Do you remember that time we went camping?" he asked her.

"Camping?" she stammered.

"Maybe we should have done something like that."

For a moment, Blossom really didn't understand what he was saying. But her heart was beating hard, the fear beat, as if a bear was hiding in some bushes waiting to eat her, which she had wondered about quite a bit on that camping trip that he was remembering so fondly!

"I'm not quite following," she admitted, nervously twisting her beautiful solitaire diamond engagement ring around her finger.

"You know. Something less formal. For the wedding."

Blossom stared at Joe, trying to comprehend what he was saying.

"Are you actually suggesting we change the wedding plans?"

"Do you think it's too late? Just us and our families and a few friends," he said, expanding a little too enthusiastically on the idea of switching out *her* wedding for camping.

She stared at him, feeling as if the man she loved so completely had morphed into a stranger before her very eyes.

Hundreds of hours of planning.

Thousands of dollars already spent on dresses

and flowers, deposits and venues, catering and live music.

"The wedding is sixteen days away," Blossom said. It sounded like her voice was being delivered in a bubble from the bottom of a well.

"I know. I'm just thinking out loud. I'm sorry."

Sorry? Had a word ever seemed so puny?

"You don't like the plan for the wedding?" she said. Did her voice sound a wee bit shrill? There was that hand rub again. This time the back of his neck. "It's a little late for that."

"I was just thinking out loud," he said, his tone aggravatingly mild.

"How can you not get this?" she asked. "It's not just a wedding. It's who I am."

He looked at the menu she had passed him.

"This is who you are?" Joe asked, picking it up and studying where she had scratched out one dessert and written in another.

CHAPTER TWO

"YES!" BLOSSOM SAID, desperately, "that's exactly who I am."

But, of course, in the back of her mind, she wasn't that at all. She was the girl standing in Ryan Paulson's living room waiting to have prom pictures done by a professional photographer.

She was the girl trying not to gawk at how gorgeous his house was.

And she was the girl trying not to notice how Ryan's mother and sister had stared at her, before disappearing, making a sense of foreboding snake across her spine.

And then she'd seen the picture on the mantel of Ryan's floor-to-ceiling granite fireplace. His sister's prom from last year. And she had been wearing the very same dress that Blossom now had on.

Feeling suddenly sick, she'd asked directions to the restroom.

On her way there, past a closed door, the voices drifting out of it. His mother and sister, distressed about the photos, about the same dress appearing on two different girls in the proudly displayed photos. His sister, her voice a bray of pure malice.

She's making that dress look trashy.

Blossom stared at Joe, feeling as if he had morphed into a stranger before her very eyes, feeling as if he had morphed into Ryan Paulson.

Or, maybe more accurately, that she had morphed into her former self: just a trashy girl pretending to be a princess.

He looked back at her steadily. "I think you're a little more than table-fired crème brûlée, or lemon chiffon cake with a blueberry reduction."

I'm not, she cried silently, though a smug voice inside her asked her if maybe she wasn't a little *less*, the girl who had grown up thinking a fancy dessert was a chocolate pudding in a packaged cup with a squirt of canned whipped cream on top.

She could feel a slow-burning fury that he— the man of her dreams—so didn't get it. The anger shocked her. Over the course of their entire relationship, she'd never been mad at Joe.

Out loud, her voice surprisingly controlled, she said, "You're trivializing what I do. It's not about brulée or chiffon cake. It's about the details. I'm extraordinary with the kind of details that move an event from mundane to magnificent. You've seen how I am about my work."

He sighed. "Right. Work."

As if she'd turned everything about their wedding into work. How could Joe not see that this wedding, her wedding—their wedding—had to be the best she had ever done, an absolute testament to her love for him?

She could feel that confident woman she had been just moments ago—or pretended to be—deflating, like a balloon with a hole in it.

The little voice was winning. *Too good to be true.*

"Sixteen days before our wedding, you decide you don't like anything about it?"

There was his opening. To tell her all the things he *loved* about their plans. Instead, he was silent.

He didn't even say he liked the *bride*.

Don't cry, she told herself.

"Maybe we should postpone," Blossom said. She didn't mean it, of course. She expected him to disagree and adamantly. Instead, he looked pensive. Her heart felt as if it was going to beat right out of her chest.

"Maybe we should cancel," Blossom said. Was that her voice? Laying down that gauntlet so cavalierly?

She saw just a flicker of something in the deep green of his beautiful eyes.

And no matter what he said next, she could never unsee that.

Relief.

He didn't want to marry her.

It felt as if everything froze around her, except the wild beating of her heart. One completely crystallized thought came out of the deep freeze.

Blossom knew what she had to do. Who wanted a reluctant groom? She had to salvage a tiny scrap of her pride.

Just as all those years ago, when she'd never found the restroom in Ryan's house, had slipped down that hallway, found the back door and walked home in those flimsy shoes.

"Consider it canceled," she said, her voice oddly firm.

Joe stared at her, stunned. "Look, that's not what I—"

"In fact—" she twisted the ring off her finger and placed it carefully in front of him "—consider *us* canceled."

Distressingly, Blossom could feel the anxiety that had plagued her for days easing. The worst had happened, right on cue. The waiting was over. Hadn't she always known good things didn't really happen to people like her?

Hadn't she always known it was like throwing a gauntlet before the gods to think she could belong in a world like Joe's?

Fear, Blossom could almost hear her mother's voice, *is like saying a prayer for what you don't want.*

Touché, Mom, touché.

A part of her, naturally, inwardly begged him

to give her back the ring, stand up and cross the distance between them, gather her in his arms, beg her not to mean it.

Just as she had hoped Ryan would come looking for her. Would call. Would *care*.

Instead, Joe, like Ryan, disappointed. He looked at the ring, astonished, and then at her.

"Are you breaking up with me?" he asked.

Did he sound faintly incredulous that *she* would be the one breaking up with *him?*

No, part of her screamed, *of course I'm not breaking up with you. I can't. You are the other half of my heart. You have made my days worth living. You are the prince I have waited all my life for.*

But it was the part of her that knew never to get her hopes up, that knew she was not princess material, that answered.

And that voice said, "Yes, I'm breaking up with you. It's over."

It was the most ridiculous impulse! And yet now she felt as if she couldn't back down. Before she could take it back, before she cried, before she threw herself upon him and pleaded with him to love her, she gathered her things—crumpled those menus and stuffed them back in her purse—and walked quickly from the restaurant, her spine straight and proud.

Part of her hoped he would come after her. Part of her hoped he would be the one who begged.

But he didn't come after her.

She wished, if she had to give in to impulses, she had given in to the one she'd had after Joe had kissed her, the one to suggest they skip lunch. It might have been trashy, the thing she always guarded against. But she would probably still be engaged! It was probably the first of many regrets her next weeks and months and years were going to be filled with.

She went right by that same construction worker. This time, he didn't even notice her. Because it was the love of an incredible man—not Bliss's outfit—that had made her beautiful. And that was lost.

Blossom DuPont was invisible again.

It was pitch-black, but when Joe touched the keypad, it lit up. In the faint illumination he could see that a hibiscus beside the door, drooping under the weight of heavy blooms, was the source of the fragrance that had been tickling at his nose.

He checked his phone for the code, punched it in, and heard the click of the door unlocking.

The keypad was a very modern addition to the door, carved of ancient, deeply grained mango wood. At his touch, the heavy door swung inward silently.

The fragrance of frangipani overtook the scent of the hibiscus and welcomed him as he stepped through into the space inside. The moon came out from behind the clouds that had turned the night to pitch, shining through an entire wall of floor-to-ceiling French-paned doors at the back of the house. Dancing shadows were cast on a room that was distinctly Old Hawaii.

Woven bamboo cloth was behind the heavy wooden beams of the high vaulted ceiling. Huge brass-and-wood ceiling fans, the blades leaf-shaped, silently cooled a space furnished in deeply cushioned antique pieces. Scattered casually about were ancient and contemporary Hawaiian art and carvings, probably priceless.

The moonlight made the wide-plank wood floors—Joe knew it be koa, which grew nowhere else in the world—glow as if they held a light. Indeed the wood was known for its chatoyancy, a property usually attributed to rare gems.

Hale Alana.

Joe had been here, to this beautiful estate, owned by his parents' oldest friends, Dave and Becky Windstorm, every single year for ten years, since his parents' twenty-fifth wedding anniversary had been held here. He'd been nineteen the first time he'd come here and the mystical allure of the Big Island had held him in its thrall ever since.

Even at the time, at only nineteen, he had known that somehow the deep enchantment of the setting had contributed to his parents' extraordinary celebration of lasting love.

Now, Joe's own celebration of love had been abruptly called off.

Dave had come down with a sudden illness while the couple had been visiting Patagonia. When Joe had received a note from Becky saying they would not make the wedding, he had not had the heart to add to their problems by telling them there would be no wedding. He was sure, in time, his parents would break the news to them.

Both pieces of news.

A canceled wedding. A devastating diagnosis.

Would his parents celebrate their own thirty-fifth anniversary? Things that had once seemed like constants now seemed horribly fragile.

"They think it's a rare kind of dementia," Joe's mother had told him, not an hour before he had met Blossom for lunch that awful, awful day just a little over two weeks ago.

They think.

Joe clung to those words. "They" had to be wrong. His dad. The most brilliant man he had ever known. The man who had always been his number one supporter, who had encouraged him to believe he could do anything. Be anything.

And then there was the other question, like a hum in the background, from the second Joe had heard the news.

Was it hereditary?

When Blossom had suggested postponing the

wedding, he'd felt nothing but relief. He needed time to find answers.

You didn't knowingly subject someone you loved to a horrible future. And, if it was hereditary, what about children? What about *their* children?

His losses felt unbearable at the moment. His dad. Blossom. Their future children. Was that why Joe had come here to Hawaii? Obviously Hale Alana had been still available. Had he been thinking he would find something in this powerful, beautiful land, where *ohana*—family—was sacred, that could reassure him about the abiding power of love?

Every single thing Joe thought about love had been tested in the last weeks and days. If his assumption was that he would find something here to bring him clarity, he could already, despite the quiet feeling of sanctuary in this room, feel the error of it.

He and Blossom had chosen Hawaii for their honeymoon because she had never been anywhere tropical. He had so looked forward to being the one to introduce her to Hawaii, and particularly the Big Island, a place of so many stunning contrasts.

On any given day, molten lava could be spilling from Kilauea, and snow falling on Mauna Kea. This island was a whole world unto itself that begged discovery, that opened the senses.

Some landscapes were dense with lush greenery threaded through with unbelievable flowers, while others were stark with the black endless seas of old lava flows.

The ocean delighted with dolphins dancing and whales breaching above water, the secret and enchanting worlds of the coral reefs below the surface.

Now, without her, without Blossom to show it to, to discover it anew with, Hawaii, that place that demanded every sense be opened, felt as empty as a yawning cavern.

Just like his life.

It occurred to Joe he wasn't going to find what he was looking for here. Or probably anywhere, for that matter. Maybe he'd just stay the night and then go home. Work had been his balm over the last two weeks. Okay, work and hanging out with his best friend, Lance, who was supposed to have been his best man.

Joe wondered what moment of madness had made him decide to trade work and those surprisingly satisfying, if somewhat drunken all-women-are-evil-so-let's-stay-single-forever discussions with Lance, for this—

The moon disappeared back behind clouds, and the room was plunged again into a darkness that matched the bleakness of his soul.

A movement, just caught out of the corner of

his eye, startled him. Too late, he realized he was not alone.

A figure, possibly taking advantage of the return to darkness, burst from behind a tall hutch in the corner of the room behind the door.

Intruder.

It seemed impossible, incongruous with the scent of frangipani and the lush, old-world serenity of the room, but Joe was being attacked.

Someone, baseball cap pulled low, charged out of the darkness toward him, a weaponized object held high. A vase?

Just before collision, Joe registered, with some relief, the slightness of frame of his attacker. A teenager, then. He caught a tiny wrist and forced release of the weapon. But his attacker managed to propel it rather than drop it. The vase narrowly missed his head, before falling to the floor and shattering. He tightened his grip on that surprisingly small wrist and heard a yelp of pain and distress.

A girl teenager.

The realization tempered his instinctive response. She was trying, with the desperation of a trapped animal, to yank her hand out of his grasp.

Thankfully, she had no hope against his far superior strength. But when escape failed, she turned and, with a warrior shout, tucked her chin, her face completely hidden by the murky darkness of the room and the ball cap. She rammed into him with surprising might.

The momentum carried them both to the ground, his hand still locked around her wrist, carrying her with him as his back hit the unforgiving, glass-covered floor. As her weight fell full on top of him, he felt the shards of glass grind into him.

Oddly, despite the shock and pain, he noted he could read her ball cap, her face completely shadowed by the brim: *True North*.

There was no accounting for minds in these situations, because his pointed out to him, with a certain languid interest, that it was a Canadian ball cap and what were the chances of a Canadian being attacked in Hawaii by someone wearing a Canadian ball cap?

For a blessed second his attacker was still, almost limp.

He thought he'd won, that she had surrendered.

But no, she'd just been gathering herself, or trying to lull him into a sense of security, or maybe some combination of both.

With the desperate strength of a wild thing, she exploded. She tried to free her hand again, and with her other she reached up and attempted to scratch his face. He closed his eyes against fingers that seemed intent on removing an eyeball, found her other wrist and held tight, thankfully before she made contact.

"Let…me…go."

She squirmed hard against him. He was still trying to temper his reaction despite the fact he was pretty sure he was now bleeding from his glass-embedded backside. His mind felt super alert and sluggish at the same time, laser-focused and yet also roaming over a large radius.

And then suddenly the scent of her hair rose above the scent of the frangipani that filled the room.

It was full seconds since she had spoken, but suddenly he registered her voice.

Something clicked.

No.

It. Was. Not. Possible.

It was just because he had been thinking about her when all this happened. It was just because it should have been him and her, Mr. and Mrs. Blackwell, coming through that door. Would he have carried her?

Thank goodness she *wasn't* here. What a terrible start to a honeymoon this would have made! To be carrying her over the threshold when a stranger came at them out of the dark.

Still, with mind both roaming and focused, Joe contemplated the ancient role of warrior protector, as *that* scent tickled his nose again.

He knew only one person whose hair had the exotic and unusual combination of lavender and lemongrass. He opened his eyes. He let go of one wrist, flicked the brim of the cap, and her face came out of the shadow.

She managed to stop her momentum midswing, which was good because she obviously fully intended to hit him with that freed hand.

They stared at each other, completely shocked. Completely frozen.

"Blossom."

Really? A man should not say a woman's name like that. Especially a woman who had just attacked him. Especially a woman who had basically left him at the altar. Especially a woman who had challenged every single thing he thought he knew about love.

A man should not say her name as if it was a blessing that had been bestowed upon him, a blessing that turned a world black-and-white back to color.

"Joe."

A man had to remember who had turned that world black-and-white in the first place.

So he stripped the tenderness from his voice, hoping in her shock, with her adrenaline running on high, that she had not heard what he so did not want her to hear.

"What the hell are *you* doing here?" he growled, letting go of her wrists.

She scrambled off him, stood up and took off her baseball cap. Her hair, which she had rarely worn loose in the course of their relationship, cascaded over slender shoulders in a luxurious, shiny dark wave.

Joe extinguished the unexpected longing of having her familiar curves pressed against him, that the simple cascade of her hair falling over her shoulder caused in him. Too easy to imagine his fingers combing through it.

Slowly, he found his feet and stood glaring down at his ex-fiancée, Blossom DuPont.

"What the hell are *you* doing here?" she shot back at him.

CHAPTER THREE

"I'M ENJOYING THE home of *my* family's friends," Joe told Blossom, heavy emphasis on whose friends they were.

In the dimness of the room, he could still barely make out her features, but he was pretty sure she was paler than usual. He reached along the wall behind him and found the light switch. He threw it.

Blossom was indeed pale. Her eyes looked huge and brown, though there was a hint of tired circles underneath them. But maybe that was noticeable because she didn't have on any makeup. Had she lost weight?

"How could you have not known it was me?" she demanded.

This seemed unreasonable, indeed. The furthest thing from his mind would have been the possibility that Blossom would arrive at their honeymoon destination on her own.

But even aside from that, he would never have recognized her dressed the way she was. Though,

like most men, he was no women's fashion aficio-
nado, he'd always appreciated the way Blossom
put together an outfit. She had an unconventional
flair that made him—most men, he'd noticed—
want to look at her and not stop.

But her outfit, at the moment, could be described only one way. It was hideous. The baggy
sweatpants were the color of a popular remedy for
upset stomachs. The T-shirt was too big, and solid
black, which might be why she looked so pale.
The ball cap was also too large, settling around
her ears. He could see why he had mistaken her
for a teenager.

Despite the outfit and the lack of makeup, he
was aware he still found her cute—very cute, in
a new and different way, like a little waif who
needed a warrior protector. He was intensely
aware of the danger of these kinds of thoughts
toward a woman who had broken his heart. These
were feelings he needed to fight as if he was
fighting for his life.

Which he was.

"How could you have not known it was me?"
he asked her back.

"I just wasn't expecting *you*."

"Ditto," he snapped.

"I thought you were an intruder," she said. Despite her attempt at bravado, he could tell she
was well and truly shaken, and he had to fight

an intense desire to gather her in his arms and stroke her hair.

There was that hair thing again. Geez, he loved her hair. It was what he had noticed first about her.

"I thought *you* were an intruder," he shot back the same words at her. "In the dark, it just looked like some young hooligan coming at me."

"Hooligan?" She looked down at herself and then tossed her hair. "This is what I really look like. When I'm not trying to impress anyone."

With hair like that, she could wear a sackcloth and still impress. Actually, a sackcloth might be an improvement over her getup.

Was there an underlying message there? That she had been trying to impress him? Their entire relationship?

If that had been her goal, she had succeeded in spades. But here they were, with her not trying to impress at all, and he was still feeling the same thing he had felt when they had danced to "Hunger" all those months ago.

It was a weakness that had to be tamed. Obviously.

"I could have killed you," Blossom offered, faintly contrite.

Her concern was hardly a declaration of love, he warned himself. People who loved you did not cancel your planned nuptials with them on the flimsiest of premises.

"There's not the slightest chance of that," he told her. "With a vase? Seriously?"

"You probably could have killed me," she decided. "By accident."

He debated telling her that his desire to kill her was so last week. But even if he said it kiddingly, she would know something of his fury and frustration with her, how her sudden ending of their relationship had devastated him.

He wasn't giving her that kind of power over him.

"Killing seems a bit extreme, but I could have hurt you very badly," he said. "What were you thinking?"

"I didn't really think. I had just gotten here when I heard someone at the door."

"It could have been the estate manager!" he admonished her.

"No, I spoke to him last week. He'd told me we would be completely alone. All the staff were given time off so that you and I…" Her cheeks flushed.

Because of what he and she might have been doing on the estate alone? On their honeymoon. That familiar heat was rising in him.

But maybe her cheeks were flushed because she had obviously misled the manager.

Whatever the reason, she attempted to cover up her embarrassment by snapping at him. "Besides, I don't think the estate manager would be creeping around in the dark. Like a creeper!"

His honeymoon night—that wasn't his honeymoon night—seemed to be deteriorating even more. A creeper?

"Look, it appears to be you who was creeping around in the dark," he said sternly, and then could not stop himself from giving her a few instructions. For future reference. So she could protect herself in the life she had chosen. Without him.

He told himself it wasn't his job to be protective of her anymore. Instructions for how to live her life were someone else's job.

And yet Joe could not stop himself.

"Why didn't you have some lights on, for pity's sake? And why didn't you hide in a closet and dial 911 if you thought there was an intruder?"

"I didn't get an international phone plan," she said haughtily. "And how would I know if they have the same emergency numbers in Hawaii as we have? How would *you* know?"

"I've been here before."

She lifted an eyebrow at him. "And your past visits necessitated a call to 911? You killed an intruder by mistake?"

He frowned at Blossom.

They had seen each other for only two months when he had known, beyond a shadow of a doubt, that she was the one.

He had never felt as alive as he felt with Blossom. The chemistry of that first night simply didn't quit. They had such incredible fun together.

He had asked her to marry him. They had been engaged for another nine months after that. Never once, in that nearly yearlong courtship, had she been like *this*. Dressed down. Sarcastic. Spoiling for a fight.

"I'm unlikely to kill a teenage girl under any circumstances, past or present."

"Trust you to be a perfect gentleman during a mugging."

She said that as if being a "perfect gentleman" was somehow a bad thing. It seemed like a flimsy reason for a breakup, but how many little irritations had to build up in a person for them to call off a wedding? Had she been stifling herself around him? She'd insinuated she had felt a need to dress to impress him. He hated it that maybe she had thought she had to change who she was for him.

He hated it that maybe calling off the wedding had been the right thing. They didn't, it appeared, really know each other at all.

"I think of a mugging as more of a street crime," he informed her.

"Let's not do semantics right now."

"Suggesting that I *do* semantics at inappropriate times? Two flaws thrown at me in two seconds. I'm glad this isn't our honeymoon."

Did she flinch ever so slightly? No, she folded her arms over her chest. "Me, too," she said.

"As lovely as this reunion is, I have—"

"To be somewhere else?" she asked hopefully.

"Uh, I have a pain in my backside."

"Are you suggesting I'm a pain in your backside?" she huffed.

"The cause of it," he said. He reached back and ran his hand carefully over a buttock. He flinched. "I'm pretty sure there's glass in me."

"You're hurt?"

He looked at her. The sarcasm was gone. She looked genuinely distressed. Easy to mistake pity for love.

"I think it's just a scratch," he said.

She was staring at his hand. "It's not. You're bleeding. A lot. Your hand is covered in blood."

He followed her gaze to his hand. It was not exactly *covered*, but he wasn't going to point that out and hear the semantics complaint again.

Before he could properly prepare himself, she had darted behind him and was inspecting his backside.

"There's quite a bit of blood," she said. "I wonder if there's more glass embedded?"

"Get your hands off my shorts!" he said tersely.

He was thinking this could only happen to him. Glass in the ass instead of a blissful honeymoon in Hawaii. The woman who used to be his fiancée trying to get his shorts off for all the wrong reasons.

"Oh, don't be a baby," she said.

A baby?

He liked the old Blossom—the one who constantly told him how perfect he was—much better.

Without warning, she yanked at his waistband. He felt air on his rear. He pushed her hands away and pulled his shorts back up.

"Let me look."

"No," he said through clenched teeth.

"I got a quick look, and it looks quite bad," she said.

His ass looked bad. Just what every man wanted to hear on his honeymoon. Except it wasn't his honeymoon.

Which did not make his ass looking bad feel any better. At all.

"You're going to have to let me look at it," she told him.

"No."

"For first aid purposes!"

"You are not going to administer first aid to my backside," he said brusquely.

Especially not on the night that they should have been in each other's arms exploring the complete world of being husband and wife.

"Oh, stop," Blossom said. "It's not like it's something I haven't seen before. And I think it's going to be hard for you to administer to that area yourself. Unless you want to go to the hospital?"

"It's just a scratch."

"I looked at it, and I'm telling you, no, it isn't. Multiple punctures. How are you going to pluck glass out of your own ass?"

When Joe had woken up this morning, it never occurred to him he might be contemplating such a question before the end of the day. And never in a million years would he have thought that question would be coming from his ex.

He did not like surprises.

He did not like things out of his control. No wonder the last two weeks had been so utterly miserable! It wasn't just the loss of Blossom…it was also the loss of feeling as if the world was a predictable place.

"I'll look after it," Blossom said soothingly, "and then you can go, though I think you're going to have an uncomfortable trip home."

Trip home? Considering that just seconds ago Joe had decided he would probably only stay the night, he suddenly felt as if a stick of dynamite couldn't remove him from Hale Alana.

"I'm not leaving," he said coolly, making a manly effort not to reach back and see if he couldn't staunch the pain with a bit of a rub. "I think you're the one who is going to have to leave."

He folded his arms in front of him.

"Well, I can't."

She folded her arms in front of her.

He lifted an eyebrow at her.

"Unlike some of us," she said, "I live in the real world."

"What's that supposed to mean?"

"I don't have access to your company's private jet. I can't flit around the world at will."

Now would be a nice time to deny he had come on the jet, but she knew they had booked it to bring them to Hawaii. He thought of how different that lonely flight would have been if their world had not blown apart. If they had been together. It was possible the honeymoon would have started at twenty thousand feet.

Do not go there, he ordered himself. *And do not look at her hair.*

"I flew economy," she said.

"I don't know what that means."

"You wouldn't."

"I know what flying economy means," he said with elaborate patience, "I don't know what it means in terms of your leaving."

"In the real world, you can't just rebook tickets without paying a financial penalty. It's usually worth more than the original flight, which was worth plenty booked on such short notice. So, I'm staying."

"You're going to have a honeymoon by yourself?" he asked incredulously.

"Is that what you're doing? Having a honeymoon?" she shot back. "Because I wouldn't call it that. After the wedding has been called off. By the way, canceling a wedding is just as much work as having it in the first place. Maybe more. I'm exhausted and I need a rest. I deserve a rest, in fact."

Was she actually acting resentful of *him?*

"You're saying that as if I called off the wedding," he said, his voice tight. "And that's not how I recall it. At all."

"Funny. I don't remember you voicing any objections."

Joe thought again, astounded in the worst possible way, that they had been together eleven months, most of those as an engaged couple. In that time, they had never—not even once—raised their voices to each other. This woman with the snapping eyes and *that* tone was a complete stranger to him.

Why did this new side of Blossom seem like a rather intriguing development?

Not that he'd ever let her know that.

"Okay," he said, with what he could muster for dignity and because the pain was becoming quite acute. "You can look."

"This isn't quite the introduction I was expecting to paradise," Blossom said to Joe, joining him as they searched Hale Alana for a first aid kit.

There was no doubt in her mind that this *was* paradise. Though the Big Island had been mostly wrapped in darkness as she was whisked to the estate in a cab, and she'd been totally exhausted from her travels, Hale Alana had pierced that exhaustion.

It was part of why she had not turned on the lights after she had stepped in the door, letting the feel of the place soak into her.

Fragrant, silent, calm, and yet oddly and beautifully *sensual*. She was aware of that now, as they went through the magnificent house. The very air around her soft and warm and moist, like a kiss.

Or maybe it was her close proximity to Joe that was making her every sense feel alive and tingly.

And also way too aware of how she looked.

She had left all those incredible honeymoon outfits that she and Bliss had chosen together behind. Just looking at them had been too painful. Well, almost all of them. She had packed a few bikinis.

And then dressed sensibly for her travels. Who needed to impress a bunch of strangers? And so she had arrived in Hawaii rumpled and wrinkled, her messy hair hidden by a ball cap. She had seen the shock in Joe's face when he had taken in that outfit.

Blossom realized it was the first time he had

actually seen her, not her dressed up the way Bliss thought she should dress for him.

Joe, naturally, looked amazing. No dressed-down, travel-weary look for him. In fact, he looked, as always, totally ready for a men's magazine cover shoot.

This evening, fresh off his jet, he was modeling tropical casual. He was wearing pressed khaki shorts and a solid navy blue shirt. The shorts showed off the long length of powerful legs, and the shirt molded his chest and the swell of bicep muscles. She felt a renegade longing to lay her hand on that familiar chest, to feel his heart beating beneath her fingertips.

His feet were in sandals, and she refused to look at them, in case she remembered kissing each of those toes individually.

His hair was only ever so faintly ruffled from his travels and he had more beard than normal, but even that was becoming on him.

Blossom surreptitiously studied his face for signs of heartbreak—bags under his eyes, worry wrinkles in his forehead, et cetera—but sadly, she could see nothing. Unless the grim line around his mouth counted.

When she looked at her own face over the last two weeks, she had seen utter devastation in it.

Her mother might be inclined to see Joe arriving here in Hawaii at the same time as Blossom as a gift from the Universe.

Blossom, however, thought she needed to see it as a *test*.

She could not entertain thoughts of reconciling with Joe.

The differences in their appearances or their travel wear choices might be a small thing, but for Blossom it accentuated the disparity in their worlds. Would she have been able to navigate his world at all without Bliss's help?

And if calling off the wedding had left her this devastated, barely eating, barely sleeping, barely functioning, what would it do to her if her marriage—that Cinderella fantasy she had nursed her whole life—didn't work out?

Not survivable, she told herself, and steeled herself anew to the shocking reentrance of Joe into her life on the night that should have marked the beginning of their honeymoon.

After a lengthy search for a first aid kit, they finally found it prominently displayed in a white cabinet with a red cross on it by the backyard pool.

If it could be called a backyard. Blossom recalled that Celia referred to the senior Blackwells' backyard as "the garden."

The Blackwells also had a pool, but nothing this spectacular.

The whole area was not like anything Blossom had ever seen before, even making Blackwell seniors' back garden and pool seem modest in comparison.

The entire wall of windows on the back of the house folded back, accordion style, so that the inside of the house suddenly and seamlessly blended into this magical grotto.

The pool was gorgeous, pond-shaped, in the middle of black lava rock. Lights under the water turned it to sapphire. Above the main pool was a smaller one, which she assumed was a hot tub. She could not imagine anyone using a hot tub in Hawaii, but still the mist rising off it added to the ambience, and for some reason reminded her she was on an island with an active volcano.

A waterfall tumbled between the two pools. More lights winked in thick green foliage and showed off the native hibiscus rioting with colors. The scent of flowers was absolutely heavenly.

"Let's get on with it," Joe snapped.

He threw himself down, belly first, across a large round glass table, his legs spread, his hands gripping the edges.

Blossom dragged her eyes from paradise, bit her tongue between her teeth and yanked down his shorts.

Now she was looking at him in such a different context from what she had once dreamed of for tonight—nearly her wedding night—that she had to bite back a laugh.

If anyone's life had taught them to expect the unexpected, it was hers. And always with the bizarre twist.

CHAPTER FOUR

"ARE YOU LAUGHING?" Joe asked Blossom dangerously.

Had she ever heard that dangerous edge to his voice before?

"No," she said.

"Because it sounds as if you are."

"It's not a *Gee, is this ever fun?* kind of laugh, if that's what you're worried about."

"I was more worried about a mocking of my undignified position."

That did make her giggle. Or maybe that baleful tone to his voice was making her feel edgy, and the giggle was a nervous one. "Now that you mention it—"

"Stop it."

"I can't."

"There's a difference between can't and won't."

"You've always had the cutest derriere," she said. The words were out before she could stop them.

"Not now, Blossom, I'm warning you." Joe's voice had a rasp to it that sent a shiver down her spine. It was unfair that that rasp—that danger—was so sexy.

The words had come out before she could think them through. Who was she kidding? The air wasn't sensual! It was her nearness to *this* that was sensual.

Her awareness of him was suddenly so acute if was painful.

"You'll be happy to know, it looks to be surface wounds," she told him, trying for an indifferent tone that denied the tingling sensation that was singing through her veins. The universe, for whatever reason, was upping the level of the test!

"I don't want to know what it looks like. Get on with it," he bit out.

Maybe he was just a little more aware of her than he wanted to be, too?

She found a pair of tweezers in the kit, placed her fingers carefully on his cheek to steady herself, and then dispensed with the first tiny shard of glass that was embedded. She should not have enjoyed his yelp nearly as much as she did.

"That hurt," he told her.

"Just pretend we're camping," she suggested sweetly. "You've landed in bramble bush."

"I had no idea you didn't like that camping trip we went on."

"There were things I liked about it," she said carefully.

Sharing a double sleeping bag with Joe, for one.

Being snuggled against him, under a blanket, a campfire going and the stars coming out, for another.

"But?"

"There were things that scared me, too." It occurred to her she was not used to being this honest with him.

"Like?" he prodded her.

"Having to get out of the tent to go pee in the middle of the night when there could have been bears out there. Thinking it felt kind of isolated, like an ax murderer could be hiding in the trees watching us."

He was silent for a long moment. "Why didn't you tell me you were scared?"

She was too busy trying to impress the billionaire, that's why. Because she had wanted desperately—pathetically, now that she thought about it—to like what he liked.

Which was really quite deplorably phony, and which had led him to believe she might be willing to trade out her dream day for a camping-themed wedding, instead!

"I thought you would think less of me."

If I showed you who I really was.

"Oh," he said, miffed, "thanks for the vote of confidence."

"I think it's about me."

"Yeah, right, not trusting me with your fears. Geez. No wonder I was attacked with a vase, with you thinking those kinds of threats are lurking in the darkness."

"See? There's the proof! You do think less of me."

"I don't," he said stubbornly, but she couldn't accept it.

"You do. You think I overreacted. You want a woman who is bold, not scared of everything."

"You don't have a clue what I want," he snapped. "And I'm not sure it comes much bolder than rushing out of the darkness to clobber a suspected intruder with a vase."

She was silent.

"I've always thought of you as bold," he said. "From the way you dress, to your willingness to try new things."

Now did not feel like the right time to confess Bliss had dressed her. And her readiness to try new things had been driven largely by a desire to please him.

"This is going to hurt," she warned him. She was *not* happy to be hurting him. She was *not* getting back at him for the sting of his comment that she didn't have a clue what he wanted. She was *not* angry because he had believed the illusion Bliss had created.

"The last thing didn't hurt?"

"This is going to hurt more. It's a bigger one. And more deeply embedded. I have to dig."

"Argh!"

"Be brave. Outdoorsy people put up with this sort of thing all the time."

"How would you—secretly scared of the great outdoors—know what outdoorsy types put up with?" She could tell his teeth were gritted.

Well, so were hers. That *secretly scared* was a judgment against the real her.

"There's this series on television where they drop people off in a remote location. It's called *That's Wild*. Last season a woman put a stick right through her foot. Now, *that* was a puncture wound."

As she had hoped, her chattering seemed to take his mind off the uncharted territory their conversation was moving them in, and what she was actually doing.

"Spare me the details," he moaned. And then, after a moment, "We didn't watch that together."

We.

A terrible pain filled Blossom. There was no more *we*. And there never was going to be again.

Because she wasn't brave enough to face all the daggers hidden in the cloak of love.

"Well, I watched it," Blossom said, as if she had a whole secret life Joe knew nothing about. Which, come to think of it, she did.

"When?"

He was right. If they had watched television—and they hadn't very much—it had been together. She certainly had not had time to indulge in the entire ten hour-long episodes of a series on her own.

Because last year, little old Blossom DuPont had had a super-sexy boyfriend and then a supernaturally exciting fiancé. Her time had been jam-packed with exquisitely romantic activities, and all the bold adventures he had encouraged her to go on with him.

And then her time had become jam-packed with planning a wedding.

No, it was since the breakup that Blossom had binge-watched every episode of the survival in the wilderness program *and* considered putting her name in for casting. Why not, now that she had nothing to live for? Now that she had thrown away her chance at happily-ever-after?

Over nothing, as Bliss had informed her.

Bliss who was so mad at her she could barely speak to her.

Because her sister felt she had tossed away the world's best guy. Because she was useless at work and could not handle the cancellations without crying. Because they had been planning a very expensive wedding, and Blossoms and Bliss was now scrambling to find money for it. Because of the late cancellation, very little of what had been put in place had been refundable.

"You have to tell Joe how much money we owe," Bliss had pleaded with her. "You have to."

Joe's mom and dad had graciously offered to pay for the wedding. But Blossom couldn't bring herself to call him—or them—and remind them. In her mind it would amount to begging for money.

In her mind, it would have just confirmed James Blackwell's *I know what you're up to.*

So, instead, Blossom had drained her own personal accounts and was waiting for loan approval. She shouldn't have come to Hawaii, but, on the other hand, she felt compelled to take a break from all the pressure her life was suddenly filled with. Except for the flight, there was no cost.

Well, the cab to Hale Alana, which was a long way from the airport, had added up to a fare that had nearly stolen her breath.

Hence no phone plan, an economy flight to get here, a sense that an expensive rebooking was not an option.

Not that Blossom had ever been anything but an economy flight kind of person, anyway.

Yes, being marooned in the wilderness with a single match—despite Blossom's former dislike of camping—now seemed like a viable option for her miserable life.

"That seems like a strange entertainment choice for someone who doesn't like camping," Joe said.

"There's a lot you don't know about me," she told him.

"Apparently."

"For instance," she said, "Bliss and Mom and I once lived in a car for three months."

Why was she telling him that *now* when it—

her secret life—had never come up when they were a couple? She'd been so thankful for that.

He went very still and then twisted his neck to look back at her.

"What?" he said.

Her heart was beating way too hard.

From her proximity to his adorable butt, obviously!

"Nothing," she snapped.

"Blossom—"

"Nearly done!" She sponged on antiseptic with a little more enthusiasm than was necessary and made a note to herself that inflicting pain was a pretty good way to stop an uncomfortable conversation.

She patched up the little glass scratches with Band-Aids and gauze until his butt didn't look sexy at all.

"There," she said with satisfaction. "You look just like a grandma's quilt."

Then she gave his butt a little slap, like a football player might give a teammate on the field, snapped his shorts back up into place, and moved back so he could get up from the table.

He did, swinging around to look at her. "Thanks for the patch-up job. Even if I do look like a quilt."

His eyes really were unfairly beautiful. The greens in the grotto intensified their depth and spark.

Blossom was suddenly aware her comfy travel

clothes were way too hot for this environment. He'd been here before. That was why he'd arrived dressed as he had, in shorts, ready for the warmth and humidity.

She told herself her sudden heat, and her desire to get naked and plunge in that pool, had nothing to do with Joe, his incredible eyes, and her recent close encounter with his naked bits.

"It's b-been a very long day," she stammered.

This would have been her wedding day.

She should have been married to this beautiful man with his gorgeous butt. Just touching him, no matter how hard she had tried to remain clinical, had filled her with the most unbearable longing.

Heat.

Not at all helped by the warmth of the tropical evening.

Well, she could put a lid on that. The hard truth was she wasn't married, she wasn't on her honeymoon, and even her sister—the other half of her soul—the one who should have been propping her up through this travesty, was barely speaking to her.

Her life, quite frankly, was a mess, a mess not in the least helped by Joe's sudden, unexpected appearance in the place she had hoped she could regroup. Pull herself back together.

Find clarity.

Grieve her loss and move on. Heavy emphasis on the "moving on" part.

But none of that seemed possible now that he'd arrived.

Joe had suggested Blossom leave, but she felt a strange sense—or maybe a familiar one—of not knowing where home was.

"I don't know what to do," she admitted. "Obviously, it's going to be unacceptably awkward with both of us here."

He had an odd look on his face. *Sympathy?* Maybe patching him up hadn't gotten his mind off her spilled confession as much as she thought it had.

"I don't know," he said slowly. "Maybe we can make it work. I think we just passed the awkwardness test. I mean, could it get any worse than that?"

"That was worse for you than for me."

"Obviously."

And then they were both laughing. It was just a moment, until they realized they were laughing together, and that it felt good and familiar and that maybe it shouldn't.

"We could both stay," he said, looking at her. "It is a very large place. I'm sure we can keep out of each other's way, blood-drawing attacks notwithstanding."

From engaged to staying out of each other's way. Was he telling her she could stay because he felt sorry for her? Or because he was grateful that she had rendered first aid? Or just because, innately, he was a good guy?

Whichever of those it was, it was a long way to fall from wildly and madly in love.

"I'll clean up the vase, then I'm going to bed." Blossom did a quick calculation of the time difference. It was 2 a.m. in Vancouver.

A time when people could become very vulnerable. And chatty. And say all manner of stupid things that they didn't intend to say, like *I lived in a car once.*

Why had she said that to him? No one knew about that. Except her. And Bliss. And their mom.

She was lucky she'd said that. And not *I love you. I miss you so much I feel like I can't breathe.*

"I'll clean up the vase," he said.

Joe! Quit being decent and nice!

Despite being very tired, not to mention totally discombobulated by his presence, she had a sudden quiver of apprehension. "What do you suppose it's worth? The vase?"

"No doubt it's Ming."

"Please say you're kidding."

"Okay, I'm kidding."

But she couldn't tell if he was or wasn't.

"But expensive," she said dolefully.

He raised an eyebrow at her. That raised eyebrow said more clearly than if he had spoken that *his* people did not furnish their homes with dollar-store finds.

"Geez, Blossom, are you going to faint over the value of a vase?"

"Possibly."

"Go to bed," he said, gruffly. "Don't give it another thought. I'll look after it."

Of course, she couldn't let him look after the expense of replacing the vase. She would add it to her crushing debt. But now was not the time to address it. He was right. Her legs were wobbly with exhaustion.

"Is there a bedroom I should take?" she asked him.

"Anything on this floor. I think the upstairs will be locked off. That's Becky and Dave's private sanctuary. When they're here. They have several houses around the world."

Uh-huh.

Those were his people. When she had told him about the car, he'd probably thought, *Whew, near miss. I almost married a girl who once lived in a car.*

She found her way to an opulent bedroom and threw open the windows to the night sounds. The scent of hibiscus floated in. She brushed her teeth and put on her pajamas, and then slid between cool, crisp sheets.

Blossom told herself she was never going to be able to sleep. Strange place. Strange bed. Adrenaline incident. The man who had almost been her husband unexpectedly sharing accommodations with her, but not her bed.

The ceiling fan made a distracting clicking sound, and in the distance, she could hear waves crashing.

She fell asleep as soon as her head hit the pillow.

CHAPTER FIVE

BLOSSOM AWOKE IN the morning to a riot of bird sound. It was what she imagined a jungle would sound like. One kind of bird was particularly loud, announcing the new day with a repetitive and insistent enthusiasm.

It was all quite exotic, light throwing palm frond shadows on the bedroom wall, a delightful breeze stirring the curtains, the sounds of the waves, more gentle than last night, the tantalizing smell of coffee brewing.

Considering the crazy events of the previous evening—and considering this should have been the morning after the night of her wedding—Blossom had an unexpectedly light feeling of well-being, certainly the first time she had felt that since her disastrous breakup lunch with Joe.

She told herself it was the magic of Hawaii, and not the fact that those rustling sounds in the kitchen would be coming from Joe.

The man who had almost been her husband.

She shouldn't really want to see him. But she

did. She looked down at her pajamas. They were what Bliss might call frumpa-lumpa—comfy, plaid cotton pants and a matching button-up top.

Changing would not be that helpful, since regrettably, every single thing she'd thrown in the carry-on—no paid luggage for her—reflected the wardrobe of a woman done with love.

But the decision what to wear turned out not to be necessary, because as Blossom lay in bed contemplating her options, she heard the front door open and then close.

She got up and went to her window, which looked out through fronded palms to the curved black driveway. Joe was leaving!

Today he was dressed in another pair of nice shorts, a crisp white, short-sleeved button-up shirt.

He was wearing sunglasses that made him look rather movie star-ish, and he had a bag slung over his shoulder. For a moment she thought he might be leaving Hawaii.

Considering how wise that would be if he left, and took all that tension with him, she contemplated the downward fall of her heart.

This was what she had to guard against: falling under his spell. She had to remember two of the words from the song "Hunger"—*love hurts*.

She would deliberately not think of the next line, which said it was worth all the pain.

She had admitted to Joe last night she was not the bold woman she might have presented herself as over the course of their relationship. Scared of everything, in fact.

But what she had not admitted was that she was most afraid of that.

Love.

Squinting at Joe's bag, she realized she could see a towel protruding from the top of it, and a tube of sunscreen.

He was just leaving for the day. Not forever.

But lest she give in to the flutter of her heart, Blossom reminded herself he was leaving *her* for the day. Making good on his pledge of avoidance. He got into a silver open-air four-wheel drive, backed up and pulled out of the driveway.

She watched him go and then noticed the view, which was almost good enough to take away the feeling of disappointment—that she didn't want to have—that Joe had abandoned her for the day.

The view was truly glorious. Hale Alana, and its substantial grounds, had been cut into the side of a hill, and the front-facing view was lush, ending in the ocean she had heard last night. In the distance, she could see a windsurfer dancing in turquoise waters, leaping in and out of white waves. Beyond the break, boats bobbed.

Something in Blossom sighed.

She went down the hall to the open living space and crossed it into the modern, very upscale kitchen. The space looked even more inviting in the bright morning light than it had last evening.

A huge vase of bird-of-paradise—that she hadn't even noticed in last night's excitement—was at the center of the island. There was also a bottle of what looked to be very expensive champagne. Beside that was a basket with a bow on it, overflowing with exotic fruits: pineapples, papayas, mangoes, avocados, passion fruit, tiny bananas.

In it was a white square card, addressed to Mr. and Mrs. Blackwell. She picked it up and ran her fingers over the cursive.

It was obvious, from the heft of the envelope, there was something inside it.

The estate manager had called her a few days ago. She recalled the conversation.

"Miss DuPont! Awakening House is ready for you."

"Awakening House?"

There was gentle laughter. "That's the translation for Hale Alana."

Awakening.

"All the staff has taken leave," Kalani had told her. "To guarantee your complete privacy. Complete."

Blossom had felt herself blushing. Geez, did he think people ran around naked on their honeymoons?

Would they have? She couldn't go there!

"The fridge is completely stocked, and the chef put meals in the freezer. Everyone here is so excited that a honeymoon is happening. They have gone out of their way to make sure everything is in readiness, everything is perfect."

Blossom had opened her mouth to tell him there would be no honeymoon. She had! But the words got stuck in her throat.

No one was going to be at Hale Alana.

No one would ever know if she went there. By herself. She could go there and nurse her wounds. She loved her sister, but she'd never dealt with anything entirely on her own.

She had done the kind of thing that Bliss did on a regular basis, but that she did not. Blossom had given in to an impulse.

Maybe she had even told herself it would be a shame to let all the work the staff had done go to waste.

Still, she had not considered the complication of a *gift*. Who should open that? Her or Joe? Should they open it at all? Of course they had to open it! And it would probably require some kind of response, but Blossom just didn't want to think about that right now.

She turned quickly from that display. Joe had made coffee, the bag that the freshly ground Kona beans had come from put away neatly beside the coffee maker.

She poured herself a cup and a little moan of pure delight escaped her at her first sip of what was arguably the best coffee in the world.

There was a note beside the coffee maker and she recognized his strong handwriting.

You could spend a lifetime exploring the Big Island and still not know it completely, but there are three must-sees: Hapuna beach (careful, big waves), the volcano (currently erupting), and the Hawaiian Tropical Botanical Garden.

The first two she got, completely. Joe would be a big-wave kind of guy. And as red hot as that volcano.

But a garden?

See? They didn't really know each other at all.

He'd very considerately left her a map, marked, and she gave it a quick perusal. She hadn't known the island was this big! The volcano was hours away. So was the garden, in the city of Hilo, on the northeastern side of the island when she was, according to the map, on the Kohala Coast. The closest attraction to her was the beach, which might be within walking distance if she felt energetic.

Which she did not.

With the price of cabs she wouldn't be doing too much exploring. Long, leisurely days by the pool were her idea of the best holiday, anyway. It was Joe who had been dragging her out of her comfort zone for all these months.

She turned and took in her surroundings and felt a tickle of delight. Aside from the awkwardness of both her and Joe showing up at the honeymoon accommodations, could there be a more perfect place to rediscover who she really was? Blossom loved the idea of holing up here for her entire stay.

The estate manager had promised everything at Hale Alana was in readiness to meet every need of honeymooners—though she was not going to let her mind go to what she and Joe might be doing if they were holed up here.

She saw that beside the big basket of fruit with the card was a plate with muffins and cheeses.

Joe had taken one pineapple out and cut it, and when she went over to the counter, the smell of that was nearly as heavenly as the coffee.

She picked up a slice and bit into it. She had never tasted anything so exquisite. What passed itself off as pineapple in Canada was not remotely the same fruit as this Maui-produced one was.

Of course it would taste delicious! It was practically the first food she'd noticed eating since the breakup.

"I am going to have the best day ever," Blossom told herself with determination.

Joe pulled up in front of Hale Alana. He had left in his rented four-wheel drive first thing this morning, grateful that Blossom had not been up yet. He had come here to get away from the flurry of feelings Blossom was one hundred per cent responsible for.

And yet here she was, and that flurry of feelings was worse than ever!

And so he had spent the whole day exploring out-of-the-way spots, trying with furious determination to enjoy Hawaii.

Unfortunately, the thought that he was supposed to be doing all this with *her* stayed with him stubbornly. It seemed each blossom he saw—and there were thousands of them—called her name.

If he was going to rate his enjoyment, so far, of the Big Island, it would be a perfect one on a scale of ten.

Because of *her*.

Thankfully, there was no sign of another vehicle in the palm-tree-shaded parking area in front of the estate house, so Joe presumed that Blossom must have found his note and decided to go exploring. As uncharitable as it was, he hoped she had, like him, had a disappointing time.

But was she being careful?

When he'd been here last, he'd benefited from Dave and Becky's long experience with the islands. For the uninitiated, however, this could be a dangerous place.

He'd been warned about the aa lava, responsible for thousands of cuts, sprained and broken ankles of the unwary every year.

He'd been warned that the ocean, in particular, could take a greenhorn completely by surprise. Those towering waves on some of the beaches along the Kohala Coast were awe-inspiring and also unbelievably powerful.

Joe realized he should have waited this morning and shared some of those safety insights with Blossom.

On the other hand, hopefully she had decided on a beach day and found her way to Hapuna, as he had recommended. It was the closest beach to Hale Alana and it had lifeguards to educate the unsuspecting.

But there were lots of secluded beaches you could find your way on to, and find yourself in trouble before you knew it, dragged out to sea by an undertow.

And the danger on the beaches wasn't just from waves.

A woman alone. Somewhat—at least he assumed—vulnerable after their called off wedding. With those big dark eyes, that gorgeous hair flowing down her back, and that air of crushed innocence, she could be targeted by a *real* creeper.

He realized he couldn't separate from his concerns for her, much as he wanted to. You didn't just turn off caring about someone as if it was a water faucet.

How could he possibly share a house with her under these circumstances, send her off to explore on her own, and not worry about her?

He'd come here with the express goal of getting away from all his Blossom-related thoughts!

I'm going to have to leave Hawaii, Joe thought, *and the sooner the better.*

It was the first peaceful thought he'd had since being attacked with a vase and then allowing Blossom to be his rump doctor.

Exiting his vehicle, he went into Hale Alana with a plan. He'd change into his swim trunks, grab a beer and a quick swim. From the pool, he'd call and make arrangements for the jet, and be on his way.

Relief swept him.

Maybe he should just skip the swim so he could be gone by the time Blossom got back. But the lure of the pool was too great. Besides, he still had to make arrangements with the pilot, and it was only early in the afternoon. If she'd made her way to Volcano National Park or Hilo he wouldn't be seeing her anytime soon.

He went and changed, slung a towel around his neck and picked up a beer. He noticed the back wall to the pool was wide open.

That was strange. Despite the fact Hale Alana

seemed like an enclave of complete safety and serenity in the world, Blossom had known last night, as she jumped to the conclusion of an intruder invading, that it was still part of a larger world. Surely she knew it needed to be locked up when they left?

If Blossom couldn't even do that, how could she possibly take proper precautions to protect herself as she explored the islands?

He stepped through the open doors and onto the deck around the pool.

Blossom was there.

His first reaction at seeing her was relief. She was safe! She'd navigated the hazards of the Big Island.

By herself.

Without any help from him.

In fact, she wasn't just safe. Joe was not sure he'd ever seen such a complete picture of relaxation.

Blossom was lying facedown on a lounge recliner on the other side of the pool, her fingertips resting lightly on a book that had slid off the lounger onto the deck beside her.

Joe gulped.

Her bikini bottoms were tiny and her back was naked, her hair pulled over her shoulder, the strings of her bathing suit open so that she would not get tan lines.

Okay, so no swim for him. When had she come

back? It must have been while he was changing, though he hadn't heard a car.

Curious, he went back to the front door, opened it and looked out. No vehicle. Except his.

He ordered himself to change his plan. Skip the beer. Skip the swim. Skip the heartache. Go home.

But he was drawn to her as a magnet is drawn to steel, and he went back to the doorway and gazed at her, unable to resist the opportunity to look at her when she didn't know. Even if that did make him a creeper.

She appeared to be fast asleep, a danger in and of itself, as her skin was very pale, just coming off a Canadian winter.

Joe greedily took in the roundness of her shoulders, the slender curve of her back, the way her shiny hair, exactly the same color as that Kona coffee he had brewed this morning, had been pulled off her back and cascaded over her shoulder, her bikini-clad bottom, her shapely legs.

Just a few weeks ago, she had been his to touch, to explore.

The chemistry between them had always been off the charts.

Who could have believed that all that could end, and be replaced by this: the sensation of empty longing that he had been experiencing since she had plunked that ring back on the table?

A new thought occurred to him, and it was

not a happy one. Maybe the chemistry between them, that compelling electrical force, had been so strong it had nearly obliterated everything else.

Including good communication.

Go, he told himself.

He had to go before he went too far down that rabbit hole. What had gone wrong? Could it be fixed? Was there hope?

Hope. Wasn't that the most dangerous thing of all?

He could leave her a short note.

Still, he took in the delicacy of her skin again. What kind of person would leave her to get sun-burned?

He took a fortifying swig of the beer and strode out onto the deck.

"Hey," he called, since he didn't have any intention of being accused of being a creeper again. Even if he just had been.

Blossom startled awake and flipped over, blinking. When she saw him she gave an adorable little shriek and scrambled to cover herself. With the book! Which she had to reach for, and which was barely any cover at all.

Had he hoped that would happen? After her inspection of his bottom yesterday, yes, indeed he had!

She seemed to realize the book was not exactly covering anything. Holding it in place with one hand, she reached around with her other until she found her towel. Glaring at him, she flipped it over herself. Damn her for looking gorgeous when she blushed!

CHAPTER SIX

OR MAYBE, JOE THOUGHT, it wasn't a blush. Maybe Blossom was just getting way too much sun.

The protective feeling she had always aroused in him was still there, just as if he had not been buffeted by Hurricane Blossom for the past two weeks.

Pretending as if being exposed to her familiar lovely curves and the cascade of all that luscious hair hadn't bothered him at all, he strode across the deck and took the deeply cushioned lounge chair beside her.

"Have a good day?" he asked her. He took a swig of beer.

"Excellent," she said, adjusting her towel primly. "You?"

"Excellent, as well." He took another swig.

"Good," she said. "I'm glad for you."

He was having this stilted, horrible conversation with the woman, whom just a few short weeks ago he'd chased around his bedroom until they both couldn't breathe.

"How's your…er…injuries?" she asked, her tone still maddeningly formal.

He should have made his escape while he had the chance.

"I'm sitting down, aren't I?"

Why did every word between them have this faintly abrasive feeling? He hated it. And he knew exactly where it was coming from.

"We have to talk about the elephant in the room. Are we going to talk about what happened?" he asked her quietly.

"What happened?" she asked, deliberately obtuse. "To your behind?"

"To the wedding. To us."

Blossom went very still. Joe noticed she wouldn't look at him. She was staring at the pool as if the secrets of the universe were about to be unveiled in those blue depths.

"This conversation seems at odds with staying out of each other's way," she decided, as if it was her decision alone to make.

"I think we need to talk about it, Blossom."

"I thought that was the line every guy dreaded. *I think we need to talk.*"

"I always liked talking to you," he said.

"Unless it was about crème brûlée," she countered.

"I want to understand what happened." There he was, going down the rabbit hole. Why hadn't he left when he had the chance? "I think it was about a little more than a stupid dessert choice."

He shouldn't have said *stupid* because she flinched, and then that remote look was on her face again.

"Humph," Blossom said. "If you were so desperate to know what happened, you could have called. Anytime in the last two weeks. And I hope that doesn't make it sound like I was waiting by the phone because I wasn't!"

That was said fairly defensively. As if she had, indeed, been waiting.

Joe looked at Blossom closely. She tilted her nose up, daring him to guess she'd been waiting for *him* to bridge the gap between them.

"I was supposed to call you?" he asked, his surprise and annoyance genuine. "You're the one who threw the ring at me."

A fact he had gone over, ad nauseam with Lance, who had confessed the other DuPont twin had also thrown something at him, once.

They had decided, between them, speech only slightly slurred, that a propensity to throw things no doubt ran in the DuPont family, and that Joe had had a lucky miss. And so, Lance had confided, had he, with Bliss, though he'd never even had a date with her.

"And not for lack of trying, either," he'd confessed glumly.

His glum tone indicated that, like Joe, he really wasn't that convinced of their good fortune.

"I didn't throw the ring at you," Blossom said.

"Semantics," he said, ridiculously satisfied to get in that dig.

She was quiet for a long time. He thought she wasn't going to answer.

"You seemed to have lost your enthusiasm for me," she told him, her tone controlled, "No girl, not even one who once lived in a car, wants a reluctant groom."

Lost his enthusiasm. For her? A reluctant groom. Him? Could she possibly believe that?

"You never said that before. About living in a car," he said. Now she had mentioned it twice in less than twenty-four hours.

"It's just not the type of thing a planner of exclusive weddings wants to get out."

"You think I would have told someone?" he said, stung.

"You wouldn't have told anyone? You wouldn't have been ashamed of me?"

"I don't recall you twisting things like this before," Joe said, and then quietly, "Blossom, I didn't lose my enthusiasm for *you*."

"That's how it felt to me," Blossom said. She tucked her towel in a little closer around her, as if to let Joe know how thoroughly he could not be trusted by her.

"At Essence that day, I was thinking out loud,"

he said, "about the wedding. I wasn't expecting a bomb to go off over sharing a thought with you."

Somehow, with that statement, he hoped he conveyed just how thoroughly *she* could not be trusted by *him*!

"It wasn't just *the* wedding. It was *our* wedding that I had put my whole heart and soul into."

"I know," he said, genuinely contrite over that part.

"Well, if you knew, how could you suddenly be wanting a change of plans? Quite a drastic change of plans, I might add."

He sighed heavily, gazed out over the pool.

"The wedding just seemed like…"

"The wedding just seemed like?" she prodded him.

"I don't want another bomb to go off."

"Bombs away," she challenged him.

"Okay. It felt as if the wedding was changing you."

There was the Blossom he'd fallen in love with—real, earthy, funny—and then there was the wedding planner Blossom.

At first Joe felt indulgent of her excitement and so happy to be the source of it. But then the wedding had seemed to become her obsession, bringing out perfectionism and a preoccupation with minutiae.

As if choosing between crème brûlée and

cheesecake was a decision with earth-shattering consequences.

It was partly his fault, he thought. He had made romancing Blossom his mission. It had given him incredible joy to see her wide-eyed wonder as she embraced the experiences he presented her with.

They had seen the famous rocker EJ in concert, had front row seats at the World Cup. They had schmoozed on the red carpet and eaten at exclusive restaurants. They had taken whirlwind trips to New York and Paris.

So, why did he remember that camping trip with such longing?

Because, of all the things they had done together in his mad pursuit of romancing her, somehow that stood out.

As real. Pure. Uncomplicated.

He'd been so intent on winning Blossom he'd bombarded her with all the experiences and gifts his money could buy. And when he wasn't doing that, he was exploring that electrical, all-encompassing energy between them. He should have left room to breathe.

After he had proposed, it seemed to Joe the level of complication had increased. As he watched, with a certain horrified fascination, Blossom had made it more and more about the wedding and less and less about them celebrating this crazy, wonderful gift called love.

And still, none of that had made him suggest she rethink the wedding.

And for some reason he didn't feel ready to reveal that. At all. Because the trust between them had become such a fragile thing?

His mother's voice played again in his mind. *"Under the circumstances, we can't come to the wedding."*

Blossom thought it was unfairly hard to think straight with a nearly naked Joe on the lounge chair beside her. He was simply incredibly and beautifully made. Broad-shouldered, long-legged, deep-chested, and narrow-waisted. This time his delectable behind was covered, but her mind could not forget, from her life before the bomb had gone off, what touching him felt like.

Tasting him.

Sheesh. And here she was clutching a towel to her own nakedness!

This could have been so much fun if it was a honeymoon. So much of their relationship had been pure sizzle.

But she couldn't let her thoughts go there. She couldn't. Because it was hard enough to keep her head on straight, even when she reminded herself Joe had just said very hurtful things to her! Blossom contemplated Joe's words.

The wedding just seemed like it was changing you.

She wanted to angrily dismiss those words, but in fact Bliss had said almost the same thing.

Blossom remembered that day she had stormed out of Essence. She had managed to somehow get back to the Blossoms and Bliss storefront without distractedly walking in front of a bus, though a cab had honked at her once, and not, she'd suspected, because of her cute skirt.

Seeing their storefront was like seeing a place of refuge from the battlefield. Blossoms and Bliss was a narrow, one-story building on a downtown Vancouver side street. It was crammed between two much larger buildings. It had been dilapidated, but they had nursed it along, seeing its potential and putting money into it.

Now it looked extraordinary. Their mother had done one of her famous murals on the outside of it, a huge cherry tree in full blossom, with blissful-looking birds sitting on the branches. The building looked like a sanctuary from the business of the city that swarmed around it, and that was how it felt, with their business downstairs and their cozy apartment upstairs.

She had gone in the door, and as soon as she was inside, she'd felt safe, as if someone had been chasing her. She recalled she'd shut the door behind her. And locked it.

And then taken it all in: the subtle pink cloud patterns painted on the walls, the walls covered in huge black-and-white photos of brides on their wedding days.

She and Bliss made dreams come true.

Except their own, apparently.

Bliss had been at her desk, and she'd looked up and frowned at the locked door, at Blossom leaning against it.

The frown was quickly replaced with alarm, her twin's intuition kicking in. She came around her desk and as she did, Blossom noted that they might be identical twins, but her sister looked— as she always did—ravishing.

The things a person remembered were silly, but Blossom remembered that day, Bliss had on false eyelashes. Blossom thought they looked ridiculous on most people, but her sister, naturally, had been rocking them. They made her eyes look smoky and sensual and full of mystery.

Bliss wouldn't have had to be in love for a construction worker to whistle at her.

It was when her cat, Bartholomew, had come and rubbed against her legs, that a little sob had escaped Blossom. Bliss had put her arms around her and leaned their foreheads together. Bartholomew, twisting in and out of their legs, had meowed as if the world was ending.

"There, there," Bliss had said. "Tell me what's wrong, Blossom."

"The wedding is off," Blossom had whispered.

"What? Your wedding?" Bliss had pulled back from her.

"I called it off."

"*You* did?"

Her sister was unaware it was vaguely insulting that she could see Joe calling it off, but not Blossom.

"I did."

"But why?" Bliss had wailed.

"All of a sudden he didn't like anything about the wedding. He wanted to go camping, instead."

Her sister had been silent. "You called off the wedding over that? He's just being a guy, Blossom. What guy wouldn't want to go camping instead of to a wedding?"

Her sister, much more successful with the opposite sex, would know about the behavioral patterns of men. Her, not so much.

"His *own* wedding. To me," Blossom had explained. "He was having cold feet. I could tell."

Her sister had taken a step back from her and studied her, tapping her own cheek with a fake fingernail. Like the lashes, Blossom didn't generally like them. Naturally, Bliss made the look ultra-sexy.

"But *you* called it off?"

"Because *he* was having cold feet!"

"Maybe it's you having cold feet."

Maybe it had been her! Trust her twin to know. Bliss had pulled her phone from the back pocket of her pants. She'd thrust the phone at Blossom. Every word of that conversation was etched in Blossom's mind.

"You phone him right now," Bliss had said. "Get this straightened out before it becomes something that can't be straightened out. That happens more easily than you think."

Blossom had slid sideways, away from the phone.

"No," she'd said, suddenly feeling a sudden need to resist her sister's direction of her life. "I'm not calling him. I don't want to marry him."

"You're being crazy!"

She'd known that. But she'd still had to rationalize it for her sister.

"I just knew it wasn't the wedding he had doubts about. It was *everything.*"

Bliss had looked strangely pensive, not at all as sharing in her outrage as Blossom might have expected.

"You're not taking his side!" Blossom had said accusingly.

"Does there have to be a side?"

"Yes!"

"Blossom, he got cold feet. Or you got cold feet. We're in this business. We've seen it happen a hundred times. Did you ask him why he was feeling that way? Why he felt as if, all of a sudden, he wasn't on board for a big wedding?"

"I did not," she had said firmly. "Stop looking at me like that. As if I'm the problem."

Her sister had sighed.

"You think I'm the problem?" Blossom had breathed.

It wasn't enough that her dream wedding had been snatched from her? Now her sister, the other half of her soul, the one who knew her so well they finished each other's sentences—was not getting this?

"No," Bliss said, but with just enough hesitation that Blossom felt sick.

"That wasn't a very emphatic no!"

"It's just this wedding, Blossom. It's changed you."

Now Joe was saying exactly the same thing!

"In what way?" Blossom had asked her sister.

"Weddings have always charged us up. Filled us with joy. For some reason, your own seems to be dragging you down."

"Being the bride is different than being the wedding planner."

Bliss had bitten her lip.

"Are you saying I was turning into a Bridezilla?"

"No, of course not, but I always felt the growing success of our business was because of your ability to care about people. You almost have a sixth sense about their hopes and dreams. You're the most caring person I know. And yet you didn't even ask Joe, the man you love, why he had this sudden change of heart about the wedding plans."

"It's too late for him to have a change of heart!"

"Well, you seem to have had one! This is exactly what I mean. Suddenly it's all about you."

Blossom had felt stunned by her sister's insensitive assessment of the situation. She wished Bliss would be quiet.

But none of her wishes had come true that day.

"There just seems to be this sense of urgency about you. Obsession. Panic to make everything perfect."

"Before it disappears like every other good thing that ever happened to me!" Blossom had wailed.

"Aw, sweetie, maybe this is for the best."

"Now you sound like Mom. *Everything happens for a reason.*"

"Maybe it does," Bliss had said, with a hint of stubbornness.

"It's way too soon for a philosophical take on it," Blossom had retorted. "My heart is broken."

"Hey, earth to Blossom!"

Blossom came back from that memory of her sister agreeing with what Joe had just said.

Joe was looking at her sympathetically. The last thing she wanted was his sympathy!

"Okay," she said, "so maybe the wedding was changing me. Not a problem now. Moving on."

"Agreed," he said. "Let's call a truce. I want you to enjoy your time here."

She hated it that he was insisting on being so decent. She was well aware she could get rid of that *I'm a perfect gentleman* countenance in a second. What would he do if she dropped the towel, reached over and touched his chest?

"I plan to enjoy my time here," she said stubbornly. "And I don't need you to do it."

CHAPTER SEVEN

THE LOOK JOE gave Blossom was aggravatingly level.

"Okay," he said, "you might not need me—"

Yes, I do need you, everything inside Blossom screamed, but she would not let him see that weakness, or any other, ever.

"No, I won't."

"The Big Island of Hawaii doesn't have many faults," he told her, "but this is one of them—you cannot go anywhere on this island without a vehicle. There's no good island-wide public transportation system. Cabs and rideshares are not abundant and not reliable."

"Cabs are expensive," she said. "I took one from the airport."

"Anyway, you should rent a car."

"Oh, I'm just going to hang out here," she said. "This is pretty much my idea of a perfect vacation. Sunshine, a book and a pool."

"You're not going to explore the island?"

"Maybe later."

He glanced over at her. He looked as if he could tell from her tone she had no intention of leaving the sanctuary of Hale Alana.

"You know, you could have rented a hotel room in Vancouver if you just wanted to sit by the pool with a book."

"No sunshine," she said to him.

He narrowed his eyes. She could tell things started to click in his mind. The economy flight. The worry about the cost of the vase. The noticing the cab had been expensive. No rental car.

"Look," he said, "you can't come to Hawaii and not *do* things."

"I might take a bus tour," Blossom said. She was pretty sure even a bus tour was way out of her budget for this trip, which was pretty much zero, but so far he didn't seem to have registered she was destitute. That was a weakness he didn't have to know about. She could still cling to her little sliver of pride.

"A bus tour," he repeated slowly, as if she had said something in a foreign language that he did not quite understand.

"There's nothing wrong with a bus tour!"

"I didn't say there was. Spare me another lecture about the real world."

"Consider yourself spared," she said, snippily.

"You at least have to get in the ocean."

Was he now suggesting *free* stuff on purpose?

"You can't come all this way and not at least get in the ocean. Boogie board. Snorkel."

Both of which, she was pretty sure, required expensive gear.

"Sharks," she said. It was not a weakness to be afraid of sharks, and lest he thought it was, she said, "Haven't you ever watched *Shark Week* on cable?"

"The woods are full of bears and ax murderers and the ocean is full of sharks?"

"Don't forget intruders creeping around in the dark."

"I'm not likely to forget that."

"Being cautious could be seen as a strength, not a weakness," she told him proudly.

"Uh-huh," he said, not convinced. "I hate to break it to you, but the biggest danger you're in—"

Is her poor heart, from being around him, obviously.

"Is getting a sunburn. Are you wearing sunscreen?"

Thank goodness he hadn't seen what the biggest danger really was. But then, Joe had proven himself to be colossally insensitive.

When it mattered.

"I'm good," she said. "I put it on where I could reach. I'm in the shade."

"Lots of people wreck their whole holiday here

because they do not understand the power of the sun, here, even in the shade."

"There's a fine line," Blossom told him, "between caring and being controlling."

He glared at her. "Let me see your back."

"No."

"You saw my heinie."

"For medical purposes only!"

"This is the same."

Why allow him to think she thought it was a big deal?

"Fine." Still clutching her towel to her, she turned her back to him. She felt him reach around her to get the sunscreen.

And then Blossom felt Joe's hands on her back. They were warm and strong as he applied sunscreen, unhurried, his movements slow and tantalizing. On purpose? She ached for where it all could go. She felt as if she couldn't breathe.

"How much are we out for the wedding?" he asked her.

Blossom realized Joe *had* figured out why she was pinching pennies. Probably all her efforts to hide weakness from him had been futile.

After eleven months he *knew* her. At least in some ways. Certainly, in *that* way, that his touch on her back, so familiar, reminded her of.

His rubbing sunscreen on her back was just a sneaky way of bringing up the finances casually, while distracting her.

As if he had figured out, and rather quickly, too, that a discussion of money with someone who had once lived in a car was going to be somewhat sensitive.

"Lots," she said. "We're out lots of money on the wedding."

"My parents wanted to pay for it. They wanted to give that to us, as a gift."

"I'm not accepting a gift for a wedding that didn't happen."

"Under the circumstances, I think they'd still want to pay for it."

"I don't need their pity."

"That's the wrong way to see it."

"Don't tell me how to see things."

"Holy moly, you're prickly."

Just what every woman wanted to hear from the man who used to love her and was currently rubbing sunscreen on her back in a manner that was criminally sexy.

"I'll pay for it," Joe said, as if that decided it, "if you don't want my parents to."

For the briefest second she felt so relieved, she thought she might start crying.

But then she had the most horrible thought. What if she had loved Joe not just for Joe? But because of this, too? And not just the way his hands felt on her back.

Bur for his ability to wave the magic wand of

money and make problems disappear? His ability to go anywhere, do anything, buy anything.

If she had married him, she would have never had to worry about money, again, ever. That little girl inside her, who was so terrified of not having enough, had finally felt safe.

He and Bliss had both been right. Planning the wedding had changed her. Being engaged to Joe had changed her.

And not in a nice way, at all.

Having enough wasn't a substitute for being enough, she realized sadly.

Blossom pulled away from his hands, readjusted the towel and leaned back on her chair. She picked up her book and pretended to read.

It was never too late to do the right thing. She waved a hand at him as if he was a pesky fly.

"No, don't give paying for the wedding another thought," she said loftily, her tone haughty with pride. "Apparently it was all about me, so I'll accept responsibility for it."

"I don't know when talking to you became like navigating a minefield," he said to her, tersely.

Her sister had indicated Blossom was a problem. Joe seemed determined to see her as a problem.

Blossom was not going to be anybody's problem, except her own!

"Oh, well," she said, "Minefields. Weddings.

Sunburns. Transportation troubles in paradise. Not your problems anymore."

"You're right," he said.

"If you're looking for something to be in charge of—"

"I'm not!"

"But if you were, you could deal with the card addressed to Mr. and Mrs. Blackwell that's on the counter. It feels fat, as if it's got something other than a card in it. No doubt, a wedding gift that has to be returned. You can deal with that since I've dealt with everything else."

"Whatever," he said.

He got up, took the towel from around his neck, and the phone from his pocket. He strode to the edge of the pool.

Blossom did not want to look at the beautiful, perfect lines of his back! She'd done a pretty good job of being strong so far, of driving him away, of killing any remaining affection he had for her.

But, she discovered, she wasn't that strong! She looked. She felt that awful ache of wanting him.

But she wasn't sure she deserved him.

In fact, Blossom wasn't even sure who she was anymore. This time in Hawaii was supposed to have been her time to figure all that out. It was going to be impossible with him here. Should she bite the financial bullet and book a trip home?

Before Joe surfaced, she fastened her bathing suit top, picked up her book and marched away.

In the safety of her room, she looked up flights leaving Kailua-Kona.

The soonest one was a week away. She was only here for a total of ten days, anyway. Nine now.

She was just going to have to suck it up.

Joe felt so angry with her he was pretty sure his skin sizzled when he got in that pool. When had Blossom become so unreasonable?

Some of his anger was with himself: he knew at least part of the sensation of his skin sizzling had nothing to do with anger and everything to do with touching her back.

He thought the swim would cool him off, but it didn't. He felt as aggravated when he finally pulled himself from the water as he had when he got in.

She had disappeared, thank goodness. It was very hard to think straight with Blossom around, especially a scantily clad Blossom, whom he had made the mistake of touching!

Obviously sharing space, even a place as spacious as Hale Alana, was unworkable. He picked up his phone and went into the house. A quick call to the pilot and his imminent departure would be in play.

He grabbed an apple banana from the fruit basket and then saw the envelope she'd been talking about.

When she'd first mentioned it was addressed to Mr. and Mrs. Blackwell, he'd thought it must be for his parents! He was glad he hadn't blurted that out to the porcupine he was sharing space with. He was pretty sure Blossom would have had something to say about the idea of them—as in him and her—as Mr. and Mrs. Blackwell.

"Because we aren't," he said out loud. She wasn't even in the room and he was defensive.

He ate the banana—a quarter the size of a regular banana, and a hundred times as delicious—in one bite. He tore open the envelope.

Blossom had been correct. It contained a card, which he put aside. Who wanted to read well wishes for an event—a life—that hadn't happened?

Vouchers and coupons, tucked inside that card, spilled all over the counter. He couldn't help but notice what they were as he tried to stuff them back in the envelope. Gate passes for Volcano National Park. Entry to the tropical gardens by Hilo. Admission to Hulihe'e Palace in Kona. A night swim with manta rays.

What was the best way to deal with it? He realized he had buffered himself from a lot of the pain involved in calling this thing off. He'd had his personal assistant go through the guest list and notify people on his side. He and Lance had had way too much to drink in the last two weeks.

He realized how hard it must have been for

Blossom, canceling everything. No wonder she seemed edgy. Exhausted.

Well, one thing she was not doing, on top of having shouldered a hundred per cent of what was involved in canceling? She wasn't paying for it.

He picked up his phone.

"Blossoms and Bliss," a voice answered on the other side. A voice like Blossom's and not like hers at the very same time.

He was not sure how two identical twins could be so different.

"Hi, Bliss, it's Joe."

Silence.

Of course she was going to side with her sister! She was, after all, the other DuPont twin who threw things.

He felt a little embarrassed knowing that about her.

"Don't hang up," he said.

"Joe! I wasn't going to hang up! I'm just shocked, but in the nicest way. I'm glad to hear from you."

"Look, I've had a discussion with Blossom—"

"Has she come to her senses?"

"In what way?" he asked carefully.

"Has she realized she tossed away the best thing that ever happened to her?"

As nice as it was to have someone see things his way, he felt a little taken aback that Bliss seemed to be on his side.

Because she and Blossom were extremely close,

the way twins were. Somehow, he had thought the twins would be shoring each other up, the way he and Lance had been doing. But if Bliss was on his side, who was on Blossom's side? As unreasonable as Blossom was being, she would need her sister right now. Wouldn't she?

"She hasn't come to that realization, no."

"I've tried to talk some sense into her, but she's not listening. In fact, she went to Hawaii, anyway. And didn't get a phone plan. I think she didn't get the plan so she didn't have to talk to me. Or Mom." Bliss paused. "How is it you've had a discussion with her?"

"Um, I ran into her."

"Ran into her? She's in Hawaii."

"I happen to…er…be in Hawaii, too."

"You're in Hawaii together?" Bliss breathed.

"No. Not really. Not together. I mean it was an accident. We're in the same place, but—"

"She can't see that's Fate?"

"Apparently not," he said, a little dryly.

"She's being unreasonable!"

He realized he was not the least bit comfortable discussing Blossom behind her back, with her sister. Though it had been another matter with Lance, now he felt guilty about that. As if he'd betrayed Blossom, and not the other way around.

How had everything Blossom become so complicated?

"I just called because Blossom kind of indicated the wedding had some outstanding items."

Bliss sighed heavily. "You're not kidding."

"I want to pay for those."

"Thank goodness!" Bliss said.

At least someone appreciated him. Bliss seemed so reasonable. It was too bad he knew she liked to throw things.

"That wasn't exactly Blossom's reaction," he admitted, "but I'm going to give you my assistant's number, and you can give her the details. I want to pay for the whole thing. Whatever's left owing and a reimbursement of whatever your business has into it."

Joe realized this—solving financial problems, doing business—was exactly in his wheelhouse. After feeling off balance ever since running into Blossom last night, it felt good to take charge.

"I can't thank you enough. I wasn't sure what we were going to do. She's waiting for loan approval, but…"

Loan approval? Joe closed his eyes. Really? Blossom was that stubborn that she'd ruin herself to make a point?

"Don't tell Blossom," he warned Bliss.

"A secret," she said gleefully, and then became somber. "Secrets don't make for very good relationships."

"We aren't in one anymore, so that's not a problem. Plus, I'm sure she's going to find out eventually, but hopefully I'll be out of range when she does."

"Joe?"

"Yeah?"

"I think Blossom might sabotage things when they're going too well. She doesn't believe good things can happen to her," Bliss told him softly. "She's afraid to hope."

Joe let that sink in. Blossom was afraid to hope.

"Anyway, thanks again, Joe. You're a really good guy."

Leave it at that, he thought, but then he didn't. "You know who else is a really good guy?"

"No," Bliss said lightly. "Who?"

"Lance."

Why had he said that? No one would appreciate it less than Lance. They had already decided, between the two of them, that women who threw things were bad news.

Even though, as Blossom had pointed out, she hadn't really *thrown* the ring at him. It had just felt as if she had, as if that returned ring had hit him with the force of a ninety-mile-an-hour baseball straight to the chest.

Then he realized why he had entered the cringe-worthy arena of standing up for his friend to the woman who had spurned him.

Because, unlike Blossom, and with all the evidence pointing in the direction of it being a foolish belief, Joe Blackwell still thought maybe people should give love a chance.

Not him, naturally.

Other people.

CHAPTER EIGHT

NOT JOE, THOUGH. For himself, he had come to the realization that hope was the most dangerous thing. Yet still—

He mulled over Bliss's final words long after he had hung up the phone and eaten several more apple bananas.

All this time together and he hadn't known that?

Call the pilot, he ordered himself.

But he didn't. He contemplated Bliss's revelation that Blossom did not believe good things could happen to her. That she *sabotaged* things when life was going too well.

His attention was drawn back to the card. It was a reproduction of a painting of a silhouette of a man and a woman sitting side by side on a beach, looking over the waves, bathed in the light of the setting sun.

It was a perfect card for honeymooners.

But it also reminded Joe of the time he and Blossom had gone camping. Reluctantly, he opened the card, bracing himself for the pain of the well wishes.

Inside was a message, hand-done in calligraphy. It was signed by Kalani and all the staff of Hale Alana. Joe read the message, and then read it again, slowly.

Maybe Blossom didn't want to marry him anymore, this woman whom he had loved, who had morphed into a stranger.

But he suddenly had a feeling it had less to do with him suggesting they rethink the wedding and more to do with a history she had hinted at and that Bliss had also just alluded to.

So, maybe, despite his own misgivings about getting married because of his fears over his father's diagnosis, he wouldn't leave. He'd take the words in the card as an invitation to see differently, to be better. He looked at the card again.

Bliss had asked if Blossom couldn't see Fate might have had a hand in both Joe and Blossom ending up in Hawaii.

He was not sure he believed in Fate, but he was not sure it was something you wanted to scoff at, either.

Joe considered the message of the card. He could delay leaving by a day, couldn't he? Just to make sure Blossom didn't hide out here the entire time and never saw Hawaii at all?

Volcano National Park and the Tropical Garden on the other side of Hilo would make a nice day trip. They could stop at Punalu'u, the most famous of the island's black sand beaches, on the way there. There were almost always turtles on that beach. He had a feeling turtles would delight her. In some small way, he could show Blossom that good things could happen to her.

And just to show himself that guess what? It wasn't always all about him. He could be a better man.

He put the bottle of champagne in the fridge. He didn't think they were quite ready to toast a truce—if she agreed to one—with that. He really needed to keep his wits about him. Besides, champagne was horrible warm.

Joe picked up the coupons and the card. Feeling like a warrior heading into battle, he strode down the hall and stopped at the door of the room Blossom had chosen. He took a deep breath and knocked.

"Yes?"

Blossom, already in her hideous pajamas, plumped a pillow behind her back, tucked the sheet under her armpits, picked up the book and pretended total engagement in it.

In fact, she had not absorbed a single word since Joe had shown up at the pool.

Joe opened the door and came in. Blossom frowned at him. Her room, which had seemed very spacious, suddenly seemed too small, as if his presence was taking up all the space and all the air.

He was still damp from the pool. He also hadn't put a shirt on.

"I opened the envelope," he said.

"What envelope?" she stammered.

"The one you told me to deal with?"

Oh. That one. The Mr. and Mrs. Blackwell one. If they were Mr. and Mrs. Blackwell, they'd be in this bed together. That delicious expanse of beautiful male body would be hers to explore, to taste, to touch.

Blossom felt almost dizzy with longing.

"It had coupons in it," Joe said, as if he had no idea how distracting he was.

"Coupons?"

"Like vouchers. For all the must-sees on the island."

He came over and dropped the vouchers on her lap.

She looked through them, trying not to let what she was feeling show on her face. Which was first of all, Joe was in her bedroom, so close his shadow was falling on her. And, a very distant second, maybe she could see Hawaii after all.

"It's not from Becky and Dave, my parents' friends," he said, "it's from the staff. Some—like that night swim with manta rays—have a date on them. And they're nonrefundable."

"Oh."

"We have to go."

"We?" she squeaked. She had thought he was giving the coupons and vouchers to her, the destitute person who couldn't afford to see Hawaii. "We, as in you and me?"

There was no *you and me*. She shouldn't have to remind him of that.

Joe, uninvited, took a seat on the edge of the bed. So close! His scent—unique to him, not diminished by his swim—engulfed her, warmly masculine.

Without warning, she was swamped with memories. Of the first night they had spent together. Of his tenderness. And of her surrender.

Of a sense of being part of a force so mighty it had created the universe, possibly out of a big bang—an explosion of energy—not so different than the one they had just experienced together.

She deliberately slid away from the temptation of all that damp skin and eyed him warily.

"This is what we have to understand," he said, apparently not being rocked by memories at all, "I'm sure Becky and Dave pay the staff well, but people who work here probably still make very modest incomes. And yet they spent their money on us. Every one of these gifts is intended to deepen our enjoyment of their home, these islands."

Blossom realized her memories had left her defenseless, weak with wanting him, exhausted from trying to keep her walls up high. It was impossible with Joe sitting on the edge of the bed. Anything he asked of her right now, she would give him. Anything.

"These people," he told her, "complete strangers to us, have extended us a welcome, an invitation to enjoy their land."

It was just wrong to be disappointed that Joe was obviously intent on sharing this gift with her, nothing more.

"I don't think you want to make Madame Pele angry by refusing such a gift."

"Who is Madame Pele?" she asked.

"She's the goddess of volcanoes. The ancient belief is that she is the creator of the Hawaiian Islands. I'd like to go to Kilauea tomorrow and see her fire." His voice dropped. "With you."

"I—"

"Before you say no, I want to read the card to you."

She was astounded that he hadn't figured out she could not say no to him, not right now.

"Aloha," Joe read, his voice even more sensual for the softness in it, "in Hawaiian means both hello and goodbye.

"But it is so much more than that. The Hawaiian people consider aloha to be a spirit that asks people to coordinate heart and mind, to come back to self-knowledge in order to *always* have good feelings toward others.

"Aloha means you treat your fellow travelers on the life journey with regard and affection, that you extend warmth and caring to each person you meet."

The beauty of what he was saying, and the way he was saying it, intensified Blossom's feelings of weakness.

"I would say that's exactly what the staff has done that for us," Joe said, "Extended aloha, by getting this place ready for us, by offering us these gifts."

She gulped, humbled, as Joe continued to read.

"Aloha recognizes people are intertwined and need each other to exist."

Intertwined, she thought, stealing another glance at his very attractive, naked chest.

He seemed oblivious to her rising temperature. "Aloha also conveys the ability to hear what is not said, to see what is not seen, and to know the unknowable."

"That is a lot for one word," she said. Her voice felt like a croak.

"Isn't it?" Joe agreed. "Finally, it says, to extend aloha also means there is no expectation or obligation for a return."

She was silent. The words touched her unbelievably. She could feel something hard around her heart break open just a tiny crack.

"I cannot refuse this gift," Joe said. "Are you with me?"

At the moment if he had asked her to bungee jump from Navajo Bridge, she would have followed him, willingly, over the edge. She swallowed hard.

His eyes met hers. "If complete strangers can offer us the gift of aloha, maybe we can be open to offering that to each other."

"Maybe we can," she agreed softly, when she found her voice. "But it seems so complicated between us."

His sitting on her bed was proving that in spades!

"What if we don't try to deal with the complications? What if we just take it day by day, and see what happens? At the end of our time here, maybe we'll have a clearer idea what needs to be dealt with and what comes next."

He was offering her the remaining time here—nine days—together. It was an unbelievable reprieve from what she had thought would be a life without him. She was not strong enough to say no to that.

"Aloha, Blossom," he said softly.

"Aloha, Joe," she responded, knowing it could mean both hello and goodbye.

And so much in between.

For one second, she leaned toward that *in between*, wanting, almost desperately, to deepen the meaning. With—

Joe jumped off the bed, as if he'd read her intent. She looked at him sourly. He'd never been the one to back away from *that* before.

Still, Blossom could barely sleep thinking of spending the day tomorrow, together, and all the days after that.

Was it a second chance for them? Or were they literally, on this island famous for eruptions, playing with fire?

Before she finally slept, she realized if this was a second chance—or even if it wasn't—she had to make an effort to fix one of the places she knew she had gone wrong.

In the morning, she was up before Joe. She put the coffee on, and as the kitchen filled with that rich scent, Blossom did a quick perusal of the cupboards to see what kind of supplies they had and if they would need anything to get them through the next days.

The house, not surprisingly, was extremely well stocked. A person could live quite comfortably here for months. She felt a familiar sense of reassurance when she found a large jar of peanut butter among the more exotic tinned and dried offerings.

Joe came into the kitchen, looking so sexy, his hair still wet from the shower. They had never lived together, and he had never stayed overnight at her place because she shared the apartment over their business with Bliss.

But Blossom had stayed at his upscale, waterfront Vancouver condo many, many times. When she thought of what she missed about that, it wasn't the granite, or the floor-to-ceiling windows with their views, the extraordinary quality of the furniture, the floor coverings, the art, or that sense of luxury and arrival.

It was the lovemaking, of course, but beyond that it was this more ordinary thing. A man in the morning, his wet hair, his scent, his freshly shaved face, the way he slid a look at her, the way he sighed with simple pleasure after that first sip of coffee.

He had on gray shorts and a navy blue shirt with subtle gray palm trees in the pattern. It was an outfit any well-heeled, eighty-year-old tourist would be quite happy to wear.

It seemed really unfair that Joe rocked it. Particularly since her own wardrobe was so limited by the fact she had refused to pay extra for checked bags.

She had on a T-shirt and shorts that could be safely rolled into a tight ball. Neither of them looked *crisp*. And certainly not sexy. That look he'd slid her way must have disappointed him.

"You're up early," he commented. If he'd even noticed her outfit was somewhat lackluster, he didn't let on.

"Who can sleep? That bird! *Ooh-hoo, ooh-hoo!* Like an excited Tigger talking to Pooh."

He smiled at her description. And she missed that, too, his smile in the morning, the memory of his mouth on hers fresh, invigorating, making the coming day seem splendid with possibility.

"It's a mynah bird," Joe told her.

"Well, I can't decide if I love it or hate it."

"Me, either," he agreed, his smile deepening. "What are you doing?"

"I'm packing us lunch."

"What? Why?"

"I had this thought. That we shouldn't spend any money. Well, not *we*. You. You shouldn't spend any money."

"Why?"

"I don't know. An experiment. See what it feels like without that. I'll pay for what we need. You've always paid."

"But I liked that."

So had she, admittedly. And, sensibly, now was not the time for her to be putting out a pile of money. *Any* money. She wasn't even confident her credit card would clear.

But they had the coupons and vouchers, and she had easily put together lunch and snack items from things in the fridge. Really, if her childhood had given her any gifts, Blossom knew how to do things on a shoestring.

She wanted—needed—to know what she and Joe were if you took away the money factor? The lavishness? The luxuries? The never having to think about money?

"Okay," Joe agreed thoughtfully. "I've been giving it some thought, too."

His eyes trailed to her lips.

"I think," he said huskily, "some perimeters would be good. For instance, we should avoid sunscreen application and backside inspections."

She understood immediately what he was saying.

They needed to avoid the kind of contacts that were bound to remind them of past intimacies. Just looking at his smile in the morning, breathing in his scent, filled her with a kind of desperate longing. Last night she had almost given in to the temptation to taste the familiar tang of those full, sensual lips.

He took her silence to mean he needed to convince her.

"Don't you think it clouded everything? That fact that we couldn't keep our hands off each other?"

She was not sure *cloudy* described how she felt, at all. In fact, it seemed to her Joe's touch had always given her great clarity, a sense of being able to see into a brilliant future.

Perhaps the very fact they saw it so differently made it a wise—if annoying—suggestion. It would keep the complications between them to a minimum.

But his suggesting that touching was now off limits made a white-hot longing leap up in her. She understood Eve gazing at the apple, the lure of forbidden fruit. Not that she'd let on.

"Got it," she said casually, as if it didn't matter one little bit to her that she had to keep her hands off him. "So, let me make sure I understand the rules—no money, no touchy."

"Do you have to make it sound as if we're in a cheap bordello?"

She giggled. He chortled. And then they were both laughing, as if nothing had ever gone wrong between them.

An hour later, the tension between them still felt eased by that moment of shared laughter. With a cooler packed with all the food they would need for the day, and beach bags packed with everything else, they were in his four-wheel drive and on the highway. Beyond what she could see from Hale Alana, this was her first real glimpse of Hawaii, since it had been dark when she'd arrived.

Blossom could not believe she had nearly chosen to miss this! Her every sense was on high alert as she drank in the new and exotic sights. On one side of the highway was the ocean, and on the other, the mountains rose, spectacular, in the distance.

"In Hawaii," Joe told her, "in the context of directions, there is the *mauka* side of the road, which means the mountain side, and the *makai* side, which means the ocean side."

Blossom was astonished by both the *mauka* and *makai* sides of the landscape. Before coming here, she had pictured only lush, tropical greenery, the Hawaii of television shows and the movies, and certainly the Hawaii of Hale Alana.

On the *makai* side of the highway she caught glimpses of postcard-pretty Hawaii, beautiful oases of green palm fronds dancing with the sky, surrounding bays of turquoise water.

On the *mauka* side, Blossom could see steep, dramatic-looking mountains that looked green and jungle-like.

But in between both the sea and the mountains, the near landscape was quite astonishingly stark.

"The lava," she said, awed. "It's everywhere. It's like driving through endless fields of charcoal."

"These are old flows, actually. Eruptions created these islands. This is the youngest of the Hawaiian island chain, which is why so much of the lava has not broken down yet. It can take thousands of years for it to become the soil that creates so much lush greenery.

"Because of continuous eruptions the Big Island grows a little bigger every year. Madame Pele at work."

Blossom had always enjoyed this about Joe. He was curious and had enjoyed so many unique experiences. But he was never satisfied with superficial explorations. He always had to dig deeper. It made him interesting and knowledgeable. In this instance, it was like having a personal tour guide. She could feel something relax in her as she remembered how easy it had always been to spend time with him.

"Do you want to stop and look at it?" he asked her.

"Oh, yes!"

He pulled over as soon as it was safe to do so, and he and Blossom got out and walked out onto the lava. The black surface was attracting astonishing heat. She bent and ran her hand over the surface.

"There are two kinds of lava," Joe told her. "This kind is called pahoehoe, and it's smooth and billowy. Sometimes it looks like big lengths of giant rope. The other kind is called ah-ah. The locals joke that *ah-ah* is the sound you make if you step on it. It's very jagged. It can be extremely dangerous, and rip through skin, or even footwear."

They were soon back in the vehicle, welcoming the breeze after the heat of the lava.

"I've never been in a roofless vehicle before," Blossom admitted. "It's exhilarating."

"And here I was just thinking of putting the roof up to protect your head from the sun."

"Please don't."

"Where's your ball cap?"

"I never thought of it this morning."

He handed her his. "We'll have to get another one."

There was that ache of missing him again. Joe was always casually chivalrous. But today, Blossom told herself, she would not dwell on what they had once been.

Her New Age mother would be so proud of her.

Blossom intended to embrace every moment as if there was no past, as if there was no future.

She put his hat on her head. "Okay, we'll get a new one, but I'm buying it."

He smiled at her indulgently. "If that's the hill you want to die on."

She enjoyed the drive immensely, admitting her focus felt sharpened by her vow to be in the moment. She was feeling as if she was soaking up the warmth and the wind, the colors and sounds, through her skin. They went by Ellison Onizuka Kona International Airport, where she had arrived so late the other night. Joe told her it was named after an astronaut, who had died in the Space Shuttle Challenger.

Onizuka, he said, was from Kealakekua, a village they would pass by today. "I'm hoping we'll snorkel in Kealakekua Bay."

She loved his ease of pronunciation, the sensual sound of the Hawaiian words coming off his tongue. A few minutes later they were entering the outskirts of the town of Kailua-Kona.

"I'm a little disappointed," she said. "A strip mall?"

He laughed. "Even in Hawaii. I'll make sure you see the downtown before you go. It's a historic village and really pretty."

But then there was the advantage of strip malls, practically right in front of her.

"Look," Blossom said, pointing, "there's exactly the place to get cheap hats. On the *mauka* side. Wally Wiggles!"

"What?"

"Turn left at these lights. That's what Bliss and I call that big-chain box store that sells everything, including the kitchen sink, and cheap."

"Everything?" he said. "We should see if we can pick up some snorkels there. Do you think they'll have that?"

"Oh, I'm pretty sure."

They pulled into a packed parking lot, and Joe secured the vehicle by putting the roof up. They got out, and Blossom stared, open-mouthed, away from the store.

"Look at the view!"

"Spectacular," he agreed, and they took a moment to stand side by side appreciating it together.

The store was perched high on the slopes of the coffee-growing mountains that surrounded the village of Kailua-Kona, which they could see below them. The view was of church spires, palms, hotels, and then the endless blue of the ocean, dotted with paddle-boarders, kayakers and pleasure craft.

She sighed. "Okay. Even the strip malls in Hawaii are beautiful."

She turned to the store and glanced at Joe. Was he eyeing it with a certain wary curiosity?

"Have you ever been in one of these before?" Blossom asked him.

"I think I've been in this chain store before," Joe said.

But that answer, and his slightly dubious tone, told Blossom a great deal. A famous celebrity had once been asked about this very store, and had giggled and said, "What do they sell there? Walls?"

Joe was closer to that world than Blossom's. He had to think about it. He wasn't quite sure. He didn't even know they would have a huge sporting goods section.

This was one of the big differences between them and their worlds. In his world, shopping meant high-end stores and exclusive websites. In his world, if he needed something, he probably sent his assistant out to get it.

In her world, you stretched pennies and found bargains and made do.

But today, Blossom was determined to treat their different worlds as a wonderful thing.

Joe could share his extensive knowledge of one of the most beautiful places in the world, knowledge born of being well-traveled and wealthy.

She could share her knowledge of Wally Wiggles.

She had never invited him into this part of her life before. Strangely, maybe because there was no longer any pressure on her to be the perfect billionaire's wife, it felt like it just could be fun!

"We'll be on a strict budget," she told him. "Fifty dollars."

"Fifty dollars?" he said, aghast, "What can you get for that? A pair of socks?"

Again, there was the difference between their worlds.

"You'll be amazed," she promised him.

CHAPTER NINE

THE TRUTH WAS Joe was already amazed. Not by Wally Wiggles, but by the light in Blossom's face as she drank in the morning on the Big Island of Hawaii.

He was reminded of what he had first loved about her, beyond the exquisite chemistry. It was her incredible sense of wonder, like the look on her face when she had run her hand over the smooth surface of the lava this morning.

He'd done the right thing by staying. By embracing the message of that card and the spirit of aloha, by stepping up to be the better man.

He watched now as she paused at a dress rack under the harsh glare of the lighting in the store. Extremely colorful sundresses were on display, with elastic bodices and skinny shoulder straps and wide skirts.

But what he really noticed was that they were ten dollars, and she was hesitating.

"This one," he said, reaching by her and plucking a dress off. It was white with bold pink hibiscus blooms all over it. "Aw, what the heck. This one, too." It was yellow, covered in white frangipani flowers.

"That's almost our whole budget," she said, but she was hugging those dresses to her, like Cinderella with a choice of ball gowns.

"Let's up the budget," he suggested.

"We're barely an hour in, and you already want to up the budget?"

"Seventy-five bucks?"

She considered this solemnly.

"Okay," she finally said, as if she was signing a million-dollar real estate deal. "On one condition."

He cocked his head at her.

"I get to pick out something for you."

Joe would not have agreed to that so readily if he'd known she was going to find a five-dollar pair of shorts for him on the sales rack. They were black with pink flamingos on them. The thing was, they made her laugh, which made it five bucks well spent, even if his dignity was going to take a bit of a hit.

She went and found a change room, came out in the pink-and-white hibiscus dress.

Joe's mouth fell open. She was making that ten-dollar dress look as if it was haute couture!

She did a little twirl in front of him and her cheap dress hugged her in all the right places and swirled around slender legs.

Joe could feel his mouth going dry.

"Is it too short?" she asked pensively.

Was there any such thing?

"Uh, no, I think it's just right."

"It's not trashy?"

"Trashy? Blossom, you couldn't look trashy if you were wearing a garbage bag."

Why was she looking at him like that? As if he'd drawn down the moon and presented it to her as a gift?

"Do you think it would be okay if I left it on?" she asked. "I'd like to wear it today."

Oh, sure, be a temptress in your ten-dollar dress all day.

He wanted to tell her that volcano might be colder, that the thin cotton dress might not be the *sensible* choice. On the other hand, look where being sensible all the time had gotten them.

Not that what had gone on between them at an intimate level could ever be described as *sensible*.

He had to get his mind off *that*, a mission made harder by the dress.

"What do you think? Should I just leave it on?"

He could hardly tell her to take it off to aid him in his mission of being sensible. In what world did telling someone to take off their dress add up to being sensible?

In a change room in a public store, he reminded himself. He had to keep his head on straight. He had to keep things in context.

To her, he said, "Sure, just leave the tag on it. They can scan you at the till."

"If you're sure," she said. "What if I forget? I don't want to get arrested for shoplifting at Wally Wiggles in Hawaii."

He wasn't likely to forget she was in that dress!

"If you get arrested," he teased her, "we could just consider it part of the adventure. Though, according to the rules, I'm not sure I'd be allowed to spend money on bail."

Joe realized it felt good to tease her, it felt good for things to be lighthearted and not so purpose-driven as they had become toward all things wedding.

"Isn't that bail bondsman on television from here?" Blossom asked. "I could bypass you. I might even be on an episode!"

He snickered at the ludicrous thought. She giggled. And then something cracked open between them and they laughed together for the second time that day. But as it turned out, it was only just the beginning of the laughter.

Because next, they found the hat section.

"How about this one?" she said, picking the most absurdly large sunhat she could find. She put it on her head and sauntered by him with a hand on her hip. She winked when she went by.

"Do I look ready for my cameo on *Jails Away*?" she asked earnestly.

"Your cameo relies on you stealing a dress," he reminded her.

"Forgetting to pay for it!"

He found himself laughing, again, which was a mistake, because, encouraged into further silliness, she found a fedora-style hat for him. Instead of handing it to him, she leaned in. She stood up on her tiptoes, one leg straight, the other bent behind her, and plopped the hat on his head.

For one breathless moment, her chest brushed his chest. Really, it seemed as if it would be petty to mention the no-touch rule over such a small thing, even if it had raised havoc with his senses.

That was the problem, he reminded himself sternly, *the smallest touch from her raised havoc with him*.

Therefore the no-touch rule, a return to sanity, a backing off from that crazy-making chemistry between them.

To hide the disturbance that smallest touch had caused in him, he turned and looked in the mirror. "I think I look like a movie star."

"Which one?"

"You guess. Just a sec," he said, "I'm going to look up a quote to go with this hat."

He found one, lowered the phone, squinted at her and deepened his voice.

"A hot dog at the game beats roast beef at the Ritz," he said. "Who am I?"

She looked at him thoughtfully. She tapped her finger on her lip. "Rodney Dangerfield?"

"Ouch! That hurt!"

"Mr. Bean?"

"Mr. Bean doesn't talk!"

"Indiana Jones?"

"That's better, even if it is because of the hat and not my innate masculinity, charm and sexiness. I'll give you one more chance."

"Okay," she said with entirely false contriteness.

"Things are never so bad they can't be made worse," he intoned, tipping the brim of his hat over his eyes.

She did that tapping thing with her finger on her lip again.

"If you don't guess right this time, we get to up the budget by twenty-five bucks."

"Humphrey Bogart!" she spat out between giggling fits.

He tilted his hat at her and drawled dangerously, "You knew all along."

She actually squealed with delighted laughter. And then they were both howling with laughter, and other shoppers moving by looked at them indulgently.

"Hand me your phone." She looked something up, then handed it back. She found another wide-brimmed hat. She bent over, as if she was holding down her skirt, half-lidded her eyes and made a cute little pucker. Despite the fact there was no hat in that famous subway grate scene, of course, he knew who it was before she said a single word.

"It's someone intensely glamorous," she told him, as if he needed a hint.

And then she said, her voice extraordinarily husky, as if she was channeling Marilyn Monroe, "A wise girl knows her limits…a smart girl knows she has none."

"Huh. Mayim Bialik?"

"Who's that?" she asked, annoyed, straightening and smoothing down her skirt.

"Sheldon's girlfriend. A very smart girl in real life. Some kind of scientist."

"You guess correctly, right now, or I'm deducting twenty-five dollars from our budget!"

He crooned softly, "Happy birthday, Mr. President," and they both had fits of laughter again.

Joe realized how strangely nice it felt to just be two anonymous tourists being silly in a big chain store in Hawaii.

By the time Blossom finally chose a five-dollar white straw sunhat, they had tried on every hat in the section, done imitations of many, many celebrities and their stomachs hurt from laughing.

Moving on from the hats, she found a shelf full of reef-safe sunscreens.

She held up one that was a spray bottle for his inspection. "I can apply this myself, in accordance with the no-touchy rule."

Looking at her in that dress, her face glowing with good humor, recalling their contact earlier when she had set the hat on his head, Joe congratulated himself for coming up with that rule!

They made their way to sporting goods. There were walls of snorkels. Joe drifted, wistfully, to the better-quality ones. He picked one out and was studying it when she came over, squinted at the price on it and gasped indignantly.

She then held up one that was half the price. "Does this seem any different to you?"

"I think in some ways you get what you pay for."

"Nonsense. This is not rocket science. Two pieces—a mask and a breathing tube."

"Generally called a snorkel?" he suggested dryly.

"This is the one I got!"

He glanced at it. It was bright pink. "Is that a kids' snorkel?"

"Yes! I have a small head. I'm sure it will fit. If I get this one and you get this one—" she wagged her choice at him "—we'll still be five dollars under budget, according to my calculations."

He gave in good-naturedly and put the more expensive snorkel back.

"We need this, then, with our extra five bucks." He plucked a plasticized chart off a rack. "It shows all the fish you'll see snorkeling in Hawaii."

She definitely had to have the chart!

"What about boogie boards?" he asked, stopping to look at a few as they passed them.

"That one board is nearly our whole budget!"

"Come to think of it, they have them at Hale Alana. I've used them before. They're stored in the garage."

She beamed at him as if he had saved the world by not spending sixty bucks on a new board.

With taxes, at the checkout, they were nearly six dollars over budget. Joe actually held his breath for a moment when Blossom saw the total, wondering if she was going to put something back. He hoped it wouldn't be the other dress, since the first time in his life that he could recall, he was looking forward to seeing what a dress looked like *on*.

Blossom didn't put anything back but gathered up their purchases with glee. No single-use plastic bags were allowed in Hawaii, and she had refused a reusable one to save seventy-five cents.

"I'm starving," she told him as they made their way out of the store, and he had to keep catching items that were falling out of her overloaded arms.

He eyed the chain hamburger joint at the front of the store with longing. "I bet we could have lunch for under ten bucks."

He should have known better.

"But I brought food! Look, there's a picnic table over there, against that wall."

He fished through their purchases for his new shorts and changed into them tucked behind the door of the jeep.

Somehow he had not seen this coming: Joe Blackwell changing clothes in a bargain store parking lot. And yet, breaking out of his long-held habits made him feel curiously alive.

Or was he kidding himself? Being with Blossom made him feel alive.

A fact confirmed by her smile when she saw the shorts.

Joe said with pretend grumpiness, "I feel as if we're getting ready for a tacky tourist party."

"We are tourists," she reminded him. "I don't think you look tacky. I think you look really—" she blushed "—cute. Do you think I look tacky?"

He gulped. "No."

He didn't expand, because she didn't look cute, either. She looked damned sexy.

He grabbed the cooler and, at the last moment, the fish chart they had bought, and followed her over to the table.

And so they sat at a picnic table at the very edge of the Wally Wiggles parking lot. Blossom handed him a sandwich and he unwrapped it.

"What is this?" he asked, prying the bread apart and looking inside.

"Peanut butter."

He wasn't aware of making a face, but he must

have been, because Blossom said to him, "Oh, for heaven's sake, don't be such a snob."

"Snob or not, I'm not eating peanut butter. I'm going to get a hamburger. And don't even suggest a hamburger from Mickey D's makes me a snob."

In five minutes he was back at the picnic table with his hamburger and a large fries. Blossom eyed him balefully as he bit into his burger.

"I'm not sure I've ever tasted anything so good," he decided.

"Oh, sure. You're just trying not to be a snob. You've eaten at some of the best restaurants in the world."

He held out the burger to her. "Taste it. You tell me."

She leaned over the table and took a bite. He watched her lips touch the very place his lips had just touched and wondered how something so very simple could seem so intimate.

She tried—and not very successfully—to act like it wasn't good.

"Want me to go get you one?"

"No! It's breaking the rules," she said.

"It is, but in a very budget-friendly way."

"That's how it starts. Then next thing you know, we're five-star dining our way across Hawaii."

"We can only hope."

"We're only a few hours in. What if I started breaking your rule?"

"Oh, good," he said. "I can hardly wait."

"In fact," she said, "you've broken my rule once, so I get a free one. To break your rule."

If he mentioned she already had when she had reached up to put that hat on his head, it would seem like he'd attached way too much importance to that.

She gave his lips a look so heated he nearly choked on his hamburger.

"Okay," he said, his voice raw. "Get it over with."

CHAPTER TEN

BLOSSOM SMILED SWEETLY at Joe. "Get it over with? Nope. My rule break could come out of nowhere. Anytime. Anyplace."

He could feel tension—delicious—shivering across his spine.

"Here," he croaked, "have the French fries."

"It's okay. I really like peanut butter." She hesitated, and then she said, "When we were kids, we didn't always have much, but if there was a jar of peanut butter in our lives, I just had this lovely feeling that things would be okay."

He was silent for a minute. "I don't get why I'm just hearing stuff like this now. Living in the car. Seeing peanut butter as a lifeline."

"I got my prom dress at a secondhand store. It was such a find. Jacob Minstrel."

Something in her tone warned him this was a big deal to her. "And?"

"It turned out my date's sister was the one who had donated it to the store. Her mother and her agreed that I managed to make it look trashy."

So, that was where the concern about the sundress came from. Joe was stunned by the flash of rage he felt. "They told you that?"

"I overheard them."

"You know what that really means?"

"No. What's it really mean?"

"It looked better on you. I'm going to guess way better. You were Cinderella, she was the ugly stepsister."

"Funny you should word it like that," she said, with a small smile that lit up his whole world.

"Why's that?"

She wrinkled her nose. "Me and my princess dreams. Blossoms and Bliss is really about fairy tales."

He considered that, the underlying tone, which seemed to imply dreams came true for other people, but not for her.

"Why didn't you ever tell me these things before?"

She lifted her slender shoulder. He noticed it was turning a little pink. She needed some of that spray-on sunscreen.

"I don't like it when I hear other people talk about their bad childhoods," Blossom said, squinting into the distance, not looking at him. "Or that they grew up poor. Sometimes it seems exaggerated. It seems everybody has their poor-me story."

"I don't," Joe said. But then he thought, *didn't*. Because, suddenly, he did have challenges of the sort he had not experienced before. A broken engagement. A sick father. His perfect world coming apart at the seams.

"I know," she said, and he heard something distinctly wistful in her tone. "You know what I really longed for, growing up? A dad. I don't even know who my dad is."

Again, Joe felt as if he should have known this. On the very odd occasion Blossom had said anything about her childhood journey, she had made it sound like a fun adventure with her wildly eccentric mother.

What a sad thing it would be not to know who your father—half of you—was. He thought again of his own dad, and how, so many times in his life, he had *needed* that firm hand guiding him through the tumultuous temptations of youth, veering him away from all the traps that awaited young men.

Somehow, as he had become immersed in his own business, his dad had always been there in the background, although not playing such a big role in his life. Joe had assumed there would be time later—maybe when the grandkids came along—for the fishing trips and baseball games and holidays together.

Now, in the blink of an eye, the possibility of children, at least anywhere in the near future, had been swept from his life, and the window of opportunity to bond with his dad had been slammed shut.

Three staff members, a man and two women, arrived at the table, cutting off their conversation. Joe was not sure if he was thankful or distressed by the interruption as he and Blossom were navigating such personal territory.

"There goes your chance," he said, and she looked relieved, as if he had expected more confessions from her. He deliberately lightened the conversation up between them.

"My chance?"

"To break the rule. I was bracing myself in case when you finished eating your sandwich, you leaped across the table and attacked me. Peanut butter kisses. Ick."

She squinted at him, a look that clearly said if she decided to kiss him, peanut butter or no, the last thing on his mind would be *ick*.

"I think I'll be more subtle than that," she decided.

The anticipation tingled again.

What exactly did that mean?

Blossom turned her attention quickly to the staff, scooting down to the end of the table. He did the same. He pointed out a little sign to her that he hadn't seen before: Staff Table.

"I'm sorry," she said. "We didn't mean to take your break spot."

But in the spirit of Hawaii, the woman laughed.

"Oh, no, there's room for everyone. Where are you from?"

When Blossom said Canada, they all shivered, as if on cue.

Joe noticed Blossom seemed more the way she had seemed when he first met her. She was totally engaged with the people, her interest in them entirely genuine. Five minutes in, she knew the names and ages of all their children!

This, he thought watching her, was why Blossom DuPont was a phenomenal success in the highly competitive wedding market in Vancouver.

A quieter voice said, *And this, along with all that wonder, is why you fell for her.*

She shared the pineapple spears and cookies that she had packed for their lunch. And the locals offered them *poke*, a diced raw fish that was a mainstay of Hawaiian cuisine.

Everybody laughed at the face Blossom made when she tasted it.

The chart Joe and Blossom had bought to help them identify tropical fish was noticed lying out on the table—somehow they had never gotten around to that in their heated exchange about sneak kiss attacks and there was much good-natured discussion about the best snorkeling spots on the island.

When Blossom admitted she had never snorkeled before, one of the young men pointed below them, to the downtown area.

"Some of the best snorkeling on the island is

right there in Kailua Bay," he said. "The little beach in front of the King Kamehameha Hotel is a great place to learn. There's lots of fish there."

"Are there sharks?" Blossom asked.

"We do have sharks here, but shark attacks are very rare. And in that particular place? Impossible. The water's shallow, and there's a man-made rock wall at the mouth. The smaller fish can get through but nothing big ever has that I know of."

After their new friends had left, Blossom gathered up their things. She looked wistfully down at the sparkling waters of the bay.

"Should we change plans?" she suggested.

Joe considered Blossom's suggestion with some surprise.

Blossom was not really what he would call spontaneous—she liked everything pretty carefully controlled.

Of course, that was part of what had blown up their world. A suggestion of change. The merest hint of it!

To be perfectly honest, he wasn't averse to controlled circumstances, either. In fact, he'd seen both their aversions to the unexpected as a good thing between them, a shared common value.

That was the nature of being two businesspeople. They were both successful in their fields because of their ability to be highly structured.

But suddenly he recognized that their common liking for security had morphed into rigidity.

When had they allowed life to become so predictable? Where had all the fun gone between them?

Maybe it was never too late to find it.

Really, it was something of a miracle that both of them had decided, spontaneously, to come to Hawaii.

"What do you suggest?" he said.

"I'm hot now. I'd love to get in the water."

"Especially with no sharks?" he asked, dryly.

"Especially that," she agreed.

Joe realized, with some amazement, that they had just picnicked in a parking lot. And had a really fun time in a chain store. That Blossom was wearing a ten-dollar dress and a five-dollar hat.

How was it possible this morning shone as brightly—maybe even more so—than all the awesome things they had done together: the concerts, the sporting events, the exclusive restaurants, the whirlwind weekend trips?

"Here's to spontaneity," Joe said, even as he wondered how far you had to stray from the plan before you entered uncharted waters.

"Here's to no sharks!" she said.

The danger zone.

He glanced at her pulling her hat low over her eyes, adjusting a falling strap on her new dress.

He realized he was tense, in the best possible way, in anticipation of when she was going to break his rule. About touching.

Who was he kidding? They were already in

the danger zone. And it had nothing to do with sharks.

His vow to be a better man was less than twenty-four hours old. And already it was wavering like a mirage on a hot desert day.

As they drove down into Historic Kailua Village, Blossom thought about their conversation. She had told him about her awful prom dress. And instead of thinking less of her, he had thought less of *them*.

It was so endearing!

"It seems everybody has their poor-me story," she had said.

"I don't," Joe had said.

And that was so true, and also endearing. That was part of what she loved so much about him. Joe seemed so normal. It felt as if he could lead her there, to that place she had always longed for.

Even now, sitting beside her in the vehicle, those crazy shorts couldn't even touch how normal he was.

Calm and in control.

"The traffic is insane," she said.

"Nothing driving in Vancouver hasn't prepared me for. You have to remember this was once just a quaint and sleepy fishing village, and a summer retreat for Hawaiian royalty. This main road, Ali'i Drive, despite lots of upgrades, just wasn't originally designed to handle the huge amount of traffic it now gets."

A tiny car shot out of a parking spot and would have hit them if Joe was not so alert. He calmly put his arm out the window, folded three fingers down, and with his thumb and pinky up, wagged his wrist at the other driver.

"What's that mean?" Blossom asked.

"It's the *shaka* sign. Sometimes called *hang loose*. You'll see it's a pretty common gesture on the islands. It kind of means, we're all friends, take it easy, all's good."

"Very different than the one-fingered salutes you get while driving in Vancouver, and that you'd especially get after nearly smashing into someone!"

"The *shaka* is just part of that aloha attitude. Look how congested it is, and yet the only agitation you see is from the tourists. And they generally calm down, become more live-and-let-live, after the islands have worked their magic on them for a few days. Besides, we got left a parking spot!"

Blossom would have passed on the slot they'd been left as too challenging to get the larger vehicle into. But Joe maneuvered into the tiny parking stall with that easy confidence he did everything with.

Again, it reminded her it wasn't necessarily the big things—fancy dinners and extraordinary travels and lifestyles of the rich and famous—that she missed about having Joe in her life. It was the little things. A man fresh out of the shower in the morning. His attitude in traffic.

His innate confidence that things, large and small, would just go his way.

She hardly knew where to look first, as they got out of the vehicle on Ali'i Drive. A steady stream of both locals and tourists moved down the sidewalks. She and Joe, in outfits that had seemed wild just a few minutes ago, were now only part of a moving river of color and energy.

"This is Moku'aikaua Church," Joe told her of the enormous structure beside them, the stones black with age. There was something about Joe's easy pronunciation of the difficult and exotic Hawaiian names that was alarmingly sensual. She turned her attention, quickly, to the plaque on the gate. It was Hawaii's earliest Christian church and had been built in 1820.

As amazing as the church was, her eyes were drawn across the street from it. A building slumbered under the canopy of the biggest tree she'd ever seen.

"It's a banyan tree," Joe said, following her gaze and smiling at her. There was something so appreciative of her in that gaze. "And that's Hulihe'e Palace."

It didn't look anything like what Blossom would have pictured a palace to be. It was a large, square cream-colored building with green shutters. It kind of reminded her of Joe's parents' house, which most people would call a mansion.

A group of people sat in a circle on the lush front lawn in the shade of the banyan tree, strumming away on ukuleles. The music floated out over the street.

"The palace is one of the things we were given vouchers to see," Joe said. "Would you like to? Since we're right here?"

She felt like laughing out loud at how the day kept defying their efforts to tame it and kept escaping their plans. She loved how it seemed as if Hawaii was taking them where it wanted them to go.

Or maybe it was just exactly as Joe had said: Hawaii itself invited you to be more laid-back, to *hang loose…*

"Of course," she said. "And then I want to see the church."

It was two hours before they finally made it to the beach after their sightseeing exploration of the downtown. Blossom felt as if she was overflowing with newfound knowledge of Hawaiian culture and history.

They walked north from the church and palace, along a sidewalk beside a stone seawall. They avoided a wave that lapped over the wall and doused an unsuspecting tourist with sea foam.

"Blessed by the sea," a local called cheerfully.

They passed under a banyan even larger than the one at the palace.

Blossom could not resist stopping and gazing up at it.

"It reminds me of an elephant," she said, as cars drove under the thick curving gray branches that canopied Ali'i Drive.

Joe paused with her. "There's an even bigger one in Maui. The canopy is said to span nearly two acres, a whole city block."

"It's incredible." Would discovering something so magnificent be just as incredible without Joe at her side? She doubted it.

"Listen," he said, cocking his head. "We've found the home to all those mynah birds."

And then he lifted his hands to the branches and clapped them loudly. The mynah birds fell silent, and she couldn't help but laugh.

"Can you do that in the morning, please?"

The mynah birds started chattering again. "As you can see, it's a temporary fix."

He turned from her just as a boy on a skateboard barreled toward them. He took her shoulder and spun her out of the way.

The boy shot them a nonchalant *shaka* over his shoulder and Blossom glanced up at Joe's face and shivered at the look on it. A warrior called to protect. He'd only been out of her life for a little over two weeks, but of all the things she missed, this was one of them. That feeling of being protected.

"That counts as your touch," Joe said, letting go of her shoulder.

"It doesn't. You instigated it."

"Show a little gratitude," he said. "I saved your life."

She smiled at the overstatement. He smiled, too.

"I remember a time you did save a life," she said.

"What? No, I haven't."

"It was the fourth time we'd gone out." That made it sound as if she'd been taking notes of every single date! Which she practically had been.

"Is that the time we started to go to the Broadway show at the Queen Elizabeth Theatre? The night you got Bartholomew?"

Such a relief, somehow, that it had meant enough to him to remember it, too. He was smiling now.

"The night you saved Bartholomew. We were walking by a grate in the street," she recalled. "And I heard that sound."

"I still don't know how you heard it. That poor kitten."

It had been pouring rain, and the water had been sluicing into that grate. When they had peered inside, a little orange kitten, drenched and shaking, had stared up at them imploringly.

Somehow, in an act of superhuman strength, Joe had wrestled the grate off and, not giving one single thought to his expensive jacket or pants, knelt down on the ground, reached down into that sewer and plucked the tiny kitten out.

He was a mess.

They'd never made it to the theatre. Joe had tucked the soaked kitten inside his jacket next to his heart, and they had run back to her and Bliss's place, dried the kitten and given it warm milk, and it had curled up on Joe's chest and gone to sleep, purring heavily.

It was the first night Joe had kissed her. *Really* kissed her. Not a polite good-night peck.

He was smiling, his smile so warm, so tender, with the same remembrance as her, that it made her unable to resist what she did next.

She stepped into him. She twined her arms around his neck. And under the banyan tree, she kissed him on the lips.

She didn't care if it was a mistake.

She didn't care if it made things complicated.

But in fact, it didn't feel complicated at all. It felt as if all the traffic noises faded. Everything faded, the crowds parted around them, waves parting on the sea. What could be simpler than a world of the two of them?

She drank in the familiar taste of his lips. She drank in his scent. She drank in the texture of him where their bodies touched.

For the first time since she had given him back his ring, the empty spot within her felt filled up. She felt complete.

She stepped back from him, savoring his taste on her lips, the stunned look on his face.

"Thank you," she said, "for saving my life. And Bartholomew's. And *that* counts as my touch."

"I thought you were going to be subtle," he croaked. And then quickly tried to recover himself. "You know what that calls for?" he asked.

"What?"

"Spending some more money."

"Don't you dare!"

"But there's shave ice right over there. You can't come to Hawaii and not have shave ice."

"I don't even know what shave ice is."

"Well, then, you're about to find out."

"Okay, but I'm paying for it!" As long as her credit card wasn't refused, that was.

Why be stubborn? If he paid for it, according to the rules of their game, she would get to touch him again.

Too dangerous.

Still, when he took her hand and tugged her across the street to the shave ice stand, she didn't even try to pull away. Somehow that—his hand in hers—felt as good as the kiss. It felt so right. It felt like homecoming. For the first time since their breakup, her world felt as if she had come into possession of a jar of peanut butter. It felt like maybe, just maybe, everything was going to be okay.

That feeling, of the whole world being right, only intensified as they sat on a bench thigh to thigh under the banyan tree, enjoying their unexpected treat.

"It's delicious," Blossom decided, licking her baseball-sized shave ice. "I don't think there could be a more perfect treat than this for a hot day."

Unless you counted that kiss. That had been more perfect than this.

"I thought you were never going to pick a flavor," Joe groused good-naturedly.

"Seventy to choose from!"

"And then you choose strawberry," he said. "Really?"

"Volcano Lava is not a flavor!"

"Apparently it is and a delicious one, too." She watched his tongue do a tantalizingly slow exploration of his orange-and-black shave ice. She suddenly felt like volcano lava, as if heat was moving through her whole body in a slow wave!

Well, two could play that game. She deliberately did something with her tongue that made him draw in a deep breath. Touching wasn't the only thing that could make the awareness between them flow red hot!

He gobbled down the rest of his shave ice without looking at her again. When they disposed of their paper cones, he put his hands in the pockets of those silly shorts. He distanced himself from the growing intimacy between them by acting like a tour guide again.

"The swimming section of the Ironman starts right here," Joe told her, pointing at a narrow band of sand on the left side of the Kona Pier. "The cruise ships anchor out there and run shuttles in."

Blossom ducked into a nearby change room, and felt both self-conscious of her bathing suit and pleased about it. She was pretty sure the minuscule black bikini—that Bliss had encouraged her to buy for her honeymoon—was going to make Joe realize the no-touchy rule was going to be pretty much unworkable between them, even if he had chosen not to hold her hand again after the shave ice.

Still, at the last moment, she couldn't be bold enough to just walk out there in that. She was shy enough to wrap a towel around herself until they got to the beach. Joe was waiting for her and they walked the few steps to the beach on the right side of the pier.

He didn't offer his hand, even when they came to the railing-free steps that led to the beach.

Apparently he'd had enough of playing with volcano lava for one day.

But then, for Blossom, the pure awareness of where they were crowded out even Joe's substantial presence.

She felt the sun on her face and a gentle breeze stir her hair. Was it possible it was this beautiful land that somehow stoked a sense of sensuality and awareness?

CHAPTER ELEVEN

"It's QUINTESSENTIAL HAWAII," Blossom breathed, taking in the outrigger canoes lined up in neat rows above the small crescent of umbrella-dotted, white sand, and the little grass hut that rented kayaks and paddle boards.

But all that was only a backdrop to a grass structure that sat on a peninsula of rock at the mouth of the tiny, sheltered bay they were on.

"What is that?" she asked, awed.

"It's a reproduction of King Kamehameha's personal Ahu'ena Heiau, or temple," Joe told her. "He lived out his final days in this bay."

Again, Blossom was impressed with his substantial knowledge of Hawaii, and how his familiarity was adding to her enjoyment, even if he was choosing, since that kiss, to hide behind the tour guide persona.

"It's a National Historic Landmark, actually."

It added to Blossom's sense of wonder and her growing appreciation of Hawaii, that she was going to learn something totally new—snorkeling—in the shadow of something so old and so obviously sacred.

They laid out towels, and then Joe sat and invited her, with a gesture, to do the same. He slipped off his shirt. She was pretty sure every female sunbather on the beach suddenly went on high alert.

He took out the spray bottle of sunscreen.

"Let me do your back."

She was very sorry she'd found the spray variety, because he was able to do her whole back without a single touch. After he'd finished doing her back, he did his own, reaching over his shoulders with the spray can all by himself.

Unfortunately, that particular stretch flexed the gorgeous muscles in his arms, broadened his chest and likely made every female on the beach go from high alert to red alert in the blink of an eye.

Unaware that he was causing quite a flutter among the female hearts on the beach—and Blossom's—Joe took their snorkels from the bag and did a manly struggle with the packaging.

"Does nobody get the irony that we can't get a plastic bag to carry this out of the store, but we can have all this to dispose of?" he said, holding up the now mutilated packaging that he had freed the snorkels from.

He handed her the pink one. "Just slip the goggles on over your head. You're going to have to stretch the band. They're tight."

She did as he asked, and the goggles snapped into place. Joe moved in close to her. "Let me adjust it a bit. It's too tight. That's what you get for buying the children's one."

She shouldn't have insisted on paying for the shave ice! Because if she had let him break that rule, then she would have another rule break available and she badly wanted one right now. The scent of him, of the sun in his hair, already turning it a lighter shade of gold, the nearness of his body to her own, was mesmerizing. It begged her to just take advantage of his closeness, to just lay her hand over his heart, rediscover the warmth of him, the silky texture of his skin.

She didn't want to admit it, but maybe his no-touch rule wasn't unworkable. She had to fight these temptations. Wanting to touch him—and badly—changed the whole feeling of the day, added an unexpected tension to it.

No, wait, that had happened when she had foolishly given in to the impulse to kiss him!

Meanwhile, Joe seemed totally unaware of the war going on in her.

"You want to tug all this hair out of the way, or the goggles won't seal properly. Now, this piece goes in your mouth, and you've got it!"

She stared out from behind her goggles, as he put his own on. He looked hilarious, like a cartoon bug. She must look the same. But for some reason, while she was pretty sure the snorkel made her less sexy, it wasn't having that effect on him.

In defense of not looking sexy, Blossom dropped the towel she had been clutching to her up until this point.

Even behind the goggles, she could see the green of his eyes turn very dark. He ran a hand through his hair, and she was pretty sure it wasn't so that the goggles would seal properly.

"Follow me," he said, put the snorkel in his mouth and waded into the water, the muscle in his thighs rippling. He turned and waved her forward.

Even with all that had passed between them, her heart sighed. Her heart said it would follow him anywhere. She did not come from the same world as him—which had probably involved swim lessons and swim team—so she was not a great swimmer. But it didn't feel as if it mattered.

In fact, even if this water had been infested with sharks, she had a feeling that if Joe would have said *Follow me*, she would have gone, trusting him to know the path through the danger.

The water felt extraordinarily sensual as she entered it, warm, lapping at her gently. Was it because her senses were heightened by awareness of him that she felt so wide-open?

"That's it," he said, his tone gentle and encouraging.

What was wrong with her? If this man wanted to change their marriage plans to a chicken coop on a farm, she should have just said yes!

"Come all the way in," he said persuasively. "Perfect. Just push yourself out, now, let go of the bottom. Lie flat, like a starfish. It's salt water, so you'll be very buoyant. You can just put your face down. Okay, now bring your arms in beside you. Just flutter kick your legs."

He rolled over and showed her.

She hesitated, feeling a reluctance to put her face in the water. But then she made a decision to give herself entirely to this experience.

Blossom was not sure she'd even known how cautiously she approached most things until that caution was gone.

She laid herself out on the water and found herself floating weightlessly. The goggles allowed her to see below the surface, and the snorkel allowed her to breathe, even if her breath suddenly had the hollow sound of a space creature testing air for the first time.

She gazed, astounded, into the depths of a watery world tinged with turquoise. It was astonishingly clear. The sun filtered through it. And then she saw her first fish!

She had never seen anything like it, ever. It was perhaps the size of her fist, boxlike in shape, navy blue on the bottom, its flat top black with white dots on it. The black section was rimmed in bright yellow.

If she had not had the snorkel clamped firmly in her mouth, she would have cried a delighted and astonished *oh* at this world that lay completely hidden right beneath the calm surface of the ocean.

A school of bright yellow fish darted underneath her. She realized that Joe was right beside her, they were moving deeper, shoulder to shoulder, his skin occasionally brushing hers, reassuring, connected.

He tapped her arm and pointed. "The state fish of Hawaii, a reef triggerfish."

He must have lifted his head out of the water and removed the snorkel to shout it at her loud enough that she could hear him even with her ears partially under the water. "It's called *humuhumunukunukuapua'a.*"

The word was a tongue twister, and his voice sounded as if he was gargling. She wanted to tell him not to make her laugh, but she would have had to remove the snorkel to do so. Instead she thumped his arm warningly. He laughed, but then surrendered his duties as narrator, and they just swam side by side, utterly engrossed in the incredible experience. Sometimes he would nudge her arm to point something out to her, and sometimes she would nudge his.

The fish came in the most amazing array of colors she had ever seen. In light blue and turquoise, in purple, in pink. Some had stripes. Some had polka dots. Some had neon lines. Some were tiny, and others were quite large.

She had no idea how much time had gone by. They made several circuits of the small bay, but each time it looked different to her, and each time they saw entirely different fish.

Finally, she had to give in to the pleasant exhaustion that was making her limbs feel heavy, the faint sensation of cold that had begun to seep into her.

The warmth of the sun felt incredible as they lay side by side on their tummies on their towels on the beach.

Propped up on their elbows, they studied the plastic Hawaiian reef fish card they had purchased, their heads close together, pointing out the fish they had seen. Parrot fish. Trunk fish. Several varieties of tangs. Moorish idols. Butterfly fish.

Joe tried, several times, to teach her to say *humuhumunukunukuapua'a*, but each time it just ended up with both of them in gales of laughter.

Finally, pretending total exasperation, he gave up and laid his head on the towel, his arms splayed out from his shoulders on the sand.

He closed his eyes, and Blossom took in the sweep of his lashes, the beautiful curve of his back, the strong length of his legs.

It occurred to her she had only ever done one other thing that made her feel as exquisitely and fully alive as snorkeling did.

And that was making love to Joe.

They snorkeled again and again, until it was late in the afternoon.

"Let's just have dinner down here," Joe suggested to Blossom. "There's so many great seaside restaurants where you can watch the sunset."

Why was he doing this?

Playing with fire? Acting as if it was their honeymoon!

Without the benefits, he reminded himself sourly, *because of your own stupid rules*.

But the truth was, he just liked being with her. Blossom's wonder—her absolute delight in everything—felt like a reprieve from the life of abject loneliness he thought he had been sentenced to the day she had given him back his ring.

And now, of course, they had to contend with her stupid rule: no money. Which, he could tell just by the look on her face, she was going to bring up.

"There's a sandwich left!" she said.

"And there goes the perfect day," he muttered. "Could I at least buy some dry shorts to put on?"

She contemplated that. "If I get to pick them."

And so a few minutes later, they were settled on the wide ledge of the seawall, with what was left of the contents of the cooler for their supper. She had changed back into the cute sundress, and he was wearing a pair of bright blue shorts gaudily decorated with illustrations of nearly every fish they had seen today.

The sense of the perfect day didn't go away but deepened, as they split the sandwich, and not in a civilized way. She took a bite and then he took a bite, passing it back and forth until it was gone.

Until that very moment, Joe might have said peanut butter was one of his least favorite foods. But somehow, with her passing him the sandwich, and the sun going down, it tasted like ambrosia.

"Look," Blossom said, nodding to her left and right.

The whole world stopped when the sun went down in Hawaii. It was like a ceremony in reverence as every single person paused, gazing as the huge orb disappearing into clouds that rode the edge of the horizon. The sky turned pink and orange, and the clouds were briefly gilded in brilliant gold. The sun wallowed briefly behind them, and then seemed to plunge into the sea. In a matter of minutes, the world was plunged into darkness.

The tiki torches began to sputter to life all around them, and they packed up the remains of their picnic and put it back in the vehicle.

Then they strolled around downtown. Somehow, their hands found each other, and that increased his enjoyment of the music and laughter spilling out of the bars and restaurants on the *mauka* side of Ali'i Drive, and how the waves, silver-capped as the moon came up, sang the song of the sea on the *makai* side.

The air, soft, warm, salty, intensified the enchantment of Hawaii.

Finally, almost reluctantly, they made their way back to the vehicle. He had a parking ticket, which he swept quickly off the windshield before she noticed it and complained about spending money.

As they took the highway back toward Hale Alana, Joe contemplated how not one single thing about the day had gone as he had planned it. They had not made it to the Black Sands Beach, the volcano, or the gardens at Hilo.

Despite his no-touch rule, they had kissed. And held hands.

Despite her no-money rule, they had spent a little bit.

It was like the islands were mocking his efforts—both their efforts—to get things under control.

When they got back to Hale Alana, he forced himself to say a very circumspect good-night, with absolutely no touching!

Because if he touched her now, their worlds would ignite, and melt together, and he would take those lips that she had teased him with this afternoon. Once he gave in to that temptation, would they ever emerge for air again?

Doubtful. He reminded himself, sternly, of his mission. To discover what they had, beyond chemistry. And on a deeper level, to protect her.

What if his dad's disease was hereditary?

The next morning, he found her sitting out by the pool, drinking coffee. What was she wearing? It looked to be one of his T-shirts.

Her hair was still ruffled from sleep, and she looked really sexy in that shirt. He felt the sharp pang of memory of what it had been like waking up to her.

A man could be swamped by those kinds of memories. A man could lose all sight of his mission, his need to protect.

"You're up early," he said, joining her.

"Mynah birds. What's on our agenda for today?"

Our. Agenda.

With those big brown eyes fastened on him, he realized it was a chance to start again. They'd gotten off course yesterday, but he could do a correction today. He didn't want Blossom to miss some of the highlights of the island because he was finding her so distracting. He needed to summon his discipline. It had always been legendary.

How could it be fading in light of something

as simple as Blossom in a T-shirt, even if it was his T-shirt.

She couldn't wear that T-shirt all day!

"I was thinking we could do the circle I had planned for yesterday. Black Sands Beach, Volcano National Park, the gardens at Hilo."

"That sounds amazing," she said.

"I'll look up the weather. To see how we should dress." He secretly hoped it was going to be really cold on the volcano and really rainy at Hilo so he could avoid an outfit more tempting than the T-shirt, like her other ten-dollar sundress.

He frowned at the phone.

"Bad weather?" she asked, disappointed.

"Uh, no, another glorious day in paradise."

"Then?"

"In Hawaii, the surf report comes up with the weather report. They're expecting really high surf on the west and north shores, starting tomorrow."

"I'm not following."

"Well, if we wanted to boogie board at Hapuna, today would probably be the day to do that."

"We can do the other things tomorrow."

Something in him surrendered. Maybe a life entirely out of one's control was not going to be as bad as he thought it was.

CHAPTER TWELVE

"SHOULD I PACK a cooler?" Blossom asked. She had gone and changed out of Joe's T-shirt. Which should have been a blessing! But naturally, she was wearing the new sundress. The yellow made him aware that her skin tone was changing, kissed by the Hawaiian sun, turning to an extraordinary shade of light gold.

He did not want to think of her skin in terms of anything kissing it.

This was how far a man could fall: jealous of the sun. It sounded like the name of a song.

"It's a fair distance from the parking lot to the beach at Hapuna," he told her, trying to focus on the issue at hand, which was whether or not they were going to pack a lunch. "We'll already have the boogie boards to carry."

She tapped her finger on her lip, drawing his attention to the fullness of it. Now, he had thought of kissing her twice in as many minutes! He was determined to exert his control, at least over this.

Joe had not seen the tapping-lips thing over the

length over of their entire engagement. Because she pretty much had gone along with him!

When he contemplated that, he realized surprisingly that he did not miss her being agreeable as much as he might have thought he would.

"There's a great food concession there," he said persuasively.

"Oh."

She did not look persuaded. He could sense her tipping away from him.

"Maybe we could have a small daily budget," he suggested, "just twenty bucks or so."

Furious tapping on her lip.

"You know," he elaborated, "so we're not chained to a cooler."

Filled with peanut butter sandwiches. On the beach. Ugh. If there was anything worse than a peanut butter sandwich, it was probably a sandy peanut butter sandwich.

Though in fairness, he had quite enjoyed their shared sandwich on the seawall last evening.

"Okay," Blossom finally said, moving her finger, blessedly, from her lip. "But I'll pay. Not you."

"I think it's my turn. You bought everything yesterday."

"Huh. We've had eleven months of your turn. I think it's my turn."

"I didn't realize it was such a burden for you," he said.

"It wasn't a burden. It was wonderful. Like a fairy tale. But life isn't a fairy tale."

There it was again. That insinuation that somehow what they had experienced during their engagement wasn't quite real.

Well, what would it hurt to do things her way? For a few days? Why not see what Blossom thought was real?

Hapuna Beach was exactly as Joe remembered it—simply breathtaking. The half-mile crescent of pure white sand was consistently ranked the best beach in the United States—and in the top ten beaches of the world.

Joe was actually glad life was a bit out of his control. If they had not had this change of plan, he might have missed seeing Blossom experiencing this place for the first time.

As he drank in her wonder, he felt like it was a life-giving nectar.

The waves were absolutely perfect—three-to-four-foot swells—for a novice boogie boarder. Though it was early, the water was already filled with people, young and old, enjoying the thrill of riding a wave into shore.

They placed their things on towels in the fine sand and Blossom wiggled out of the dress. What she had on underneath it was a thousand times more beguiling than the dress! A little white-and-yellow bikini that, if he didn't know better, he could have sworn had been purchased to match the dress.

It now seemed imperative to get into the water. Fast!

But there was the whole sunscreen thing they had to get through. He, congratulating himself on his wisdom, handed her the spray bottle to do her own...which was not so wise after all. Those contortions were delectable!

"The waves seem quite high," she said with a bit of trepidation, when the sunscreen ritual was finally, mercifully, finished.

"Don't worry. We'll stay shallow. See where those kids are playing? We'll go right there."

Joe showed Blossom how to strap the board lines to her ankle, and then holding the boards in front of them, they waded out into the crashing surf.

They were soaked in seconds from the foam exploding off the waves. She looked like a model for one of those swimsuit-edition sports magazines! When they were in up to their thighs, he turned around, putting his back to the ocean, his boogie board in front of him. He gestured for her to do the same.

"Look over your shoulder," he called to her. "When you see a good wave, grab it! Right on the break. There it is!"

He held his board out in front of him, felt the wave lifting him up and at exactly the right moment, threw himself onto the board. Out of the corner of his eye, he saw Blossom doing the same thing.

She was on her belly, leaning on her elbows, her fingertips in a death grip on the front of the board.

The white crest of the wave caught her and propelled her forward.

Her mouth formed a tiny O of astonishment at the speed of the wave. And then, she was in the shallow water, tumbling off the board, laughing and swallowing seawater.

He went and plucked her out of the sand before the next wave hit her and smacked the board into her.

She didn't seem to notice she was practically melted against him in that very scanty outfit.

"How can I have lived this long and missed out on this experience?" she asked him breathlessly. Her trepidation had completely melted away. And then with a squeal of delight, she was out of his arms in a flash, running back into the waves, waiting eagerly, in the line of children, for the next wave.

Joe just watched, intensely enjoying her enjoyment. She took a wave, but grabbed it just a bit too late, and it fizzled. She caught the next one, and rode it all the way into the sand, where she was unceremoniously dumped.

She howled with laughter as he plucked her

from the sand, rescuing her from getting pummeled by the incoming wave.

"Ah," he adjusted the strap on her bathing suit. "You're losing your top."

"I think my britches nearly got yanked off, too."

He gaped at her. And then she laughed. Her laughter was amazing.

And totally contagious.

In all the time they had been together, Joe was not sure he had seen this in her. A complete letting go. A surrender to joy.

He was suddenly aware that everyone seemed to be laughing. The children. Her. Him. They had entered the zone of pure happiness.

He ran back to where their stuff was on the beach and extracted his T-shirt for her.

"Sunburn," he said gruffly, handing it to her.

"Oh," she said, pulling it over her head, "who are you trying to kid? You're protecting me from wardrobe malfunctions."

Either way, he was protecting her, and it felt, dangerously, like the job he'd been born to do.

They went back out into the waves and waited, side by side, watching for just the right one. They played relentlessly, giving themselves over to being the biggest kids on the beach. Their bliss blended into the shrieks and laughter of the children around them. The whole experience—the waves, the sun, the sand—all seemed to shimmer with an uncanny light.

They gave themselves over, completely, to the ocean.

They played and played and played. His stomach actually hurt, not from the bruising activity, but from the laughter.

Finally, exhausted, legs rubbery from exertion, they exited the water. She looked as sexy in that sopping, clinging shirt as she had looked in just the bathing suit!

She stripped it off and threw herself on her towel, still panting with exertion. He lay down beside her.

The happiness continued to shimmer in the air between them as the warm air and sea breezes dried them.

"Let's get out of the sun for a bit. We'll go get something to eat," he suggested after a while. He slipped on his shirt and she pulled her sundress back over her head. Her wet bathing suit showed through it.

He was not sure Blossom had ever looked more beautiful: her hair soaked, her face sandy, her dress transparent, her feet bare. She looked like a creature of the sea, a mermaid who had been granted a day to be human.

They walked up the hill above the beach on a paved pathway. Somehow, she was holding his hand. Joe felt so light, so carefree, from what they had just experienced he wasn't even sure holding hands would qualify for the no-touch rule.

Somehow, it just seemed as if it would be petty to mention it. Somehow it didn't seem like a day for rules. At all.

At the concession stand they ordered the famous fish tacos and then sat at a picnic table in the shade to eat them. Blossom said what he was thinking.

"I think I'm in heaven." She bit into her taco, drinking in the incredible view.

Joe, so magnificently male, was part of that view. Part of the great sense of exhilaration unfurling in her like a sail catching the wind.

At first, she noticed that a noisy group of young girls and a few mothers had taken a table not far away, only on her periphery. But she focused more on them as their exuberance increased. The table they were at was festooned with balloons and the girls were wearing party hats. Her feeling of happiness was suddenly tempered with an odd wistfulness.

"Birthday party," Joe said, following her gaze. "Do you think this would be the best place ever to have a party?"

The perfection of the day was suddenly marred. She had thought they would have children, someday. Stockings on the fireplace at Christmastime. Birthday parties. A dog.

A *normal* life.

"What was your best birthday party?" Blossom asked.

"Hard to pick just one. I remember being really young and going through a pirate phase. My mom had a themed birthday party for me. There was a couple of pirates there who had a sword fight. There was a cake shaped like a treasure chest, spilling gummy candies out of it.

"When I was ten, the folks rented a whole paintball place for the party. Fourteen ten-year-olds trying to murder each other. You would think it doesn't get any better than that, but the next year my dad got us tickets for the World Series."

Was that what his father had seen in her when he'd said *"I know what you're up to"*?

That she was the girl desperate to belong to a world where someone had trouble picking their favorite birthday party out of their memory box?

"Your birthdays must have been different?"

She started. How did he know?

"Sharing it with a twin?"

"Oh, that wasn't the only way they were different."

"What do you mean?"

Blossom said, "I don't remember a best one. Maybe a most memorable one."

"Okay, tell me about that one."

She considered this. She thought of how she had given him carefully edited versions of her life, making growing up with an eccentric mother seem as if it had been only fun, an endless adventure in unpredictability.

"I know what you're up to."

As if Joe's father knew she was an imposter. As if he was aware that there were things she had deliberately not said, and that she was just trying to use his family to improve her position in life. As if he thought she could never quite belong.

If this was going anywhere—their faux honeymoon—maybe it was time for a little more honesty.

Was it going anywhere? For as lovely as Joe was being, this man who had almost been her husband, protective and attentive, he certainly had not indicated there was a future for them beyond these few days.

"Bliss and I were turning seven," Blossom said slowly, her eyes on those carefree girls at the table next to them. "We were living in the Okanagan Valley. My mom had gotten a job painting sets for a theatre company run by hippies. We were new in town, as always, and she promised us a birthday party that would make everyone want to be friends with us. She promised us ponies at the party.

"We even advertised them on the birthday invitations. Everybody in our whole class came. That was a first.

"And then the pony lady showed up. She rattled up in a rusted trailer that looked like the wheels were going to fall off. She had eight ponies, but she was drunk before they were all saddled. And then the ponies revolted and all got away. While she threw beer bottles at them and cursed, the ponies dodged her, drank out of the wading pool and ate the birthday cake.

"One of the ponies—a little black one with a white mane and tail—knocked over a snooty girl named Beth-Anne. She had mud all over her dress."

She snuck him a look. She'd kept her tone light, as if it had all been quite hilarious.

But Joe did not look the least bit fooled. "Aw, Blossom, I'm sorry. I really am."

She smiled shakily. "You know what's funny?"

His look told her there was nothing funny about what she had just told him.

"You know how close Bliss and I are?" she pressed on.

"Of course. You finish each other's sentences. You scrunch up your noses the same. You dress the same."

She considered telling him she hadn't dressed the same as Bliss before she'd met him and Bliss had appointed herself the fashion police, but one confession at a time seemed like more than enough.

"I mean, we are different in some ways. Bliss is way more extroverted than I am. Although usually we're so much on the same wavelength that we have the same dreams at night. But you know what Bliss says when that party comes up?"

"What?"

"'*Best birthday party ever.*' She's particularly gleeful about Beth-Anne and her frilly party dress."

"And you?" he asked quietly.

"Definitely not the best birthday party ever. Not even close. What I remember is that, after that, Beth-Anne slid us looks and the other kids in the class seemed standoffish. I usually wasn't glad when my mother announced another move, but I was that time."

"I'm really sorry," he said again. As if he meant it. It didn't seem as if he pitied her. The look in his green eyes was purely empathetic.

And yet she felt that familiar need to minimize.

"Life with Mom," she said lightly, making a concerted effort to drag her eyes away from that oh-so-normal birthday party. "Always unpredictable. However, it gave me a lot of tools for dealing with the unexpected."

She could tell Joe didn't fall for her light tone, or her declaration of lessons-learned. He looked pensive. He didn't say a single word. But when he covered her hand with his own, there was no pity in the small gesture.

In fact, what was in that gesture, and in his eyes when he looked at her, was the greatest gift of all.

Acceptance.

The gift she had never been able to totally give herself.

It occurred to her she had done Joe a disservice by not trusting him earlier with some of the details of her life. She'd done a disservice to him, and to herself, as well.

Because this moment with Joe, his hand on top of hers, felt like one of the most intimate they had ever shared.

CHAPTER THIRTEEN

THAT MOMENT OF Blossom telling Joe about her seventh birthday party—and his reaction to it—gave her courage.

Not just to tackle waves and a possibly shark-infested ocean, and all manner of things unknown, but to reveal herself. To be herself in ways she had not allowed herself to be before.

"Hey," he said that night, after they had returned from Hapuna, exhausted and exhilarated. "I have another beach I want to show you."

"I can't ride one more wave. Okay. Maybe one."

"This is a different kind of beach. I thought we could get supper down there. There's a couple of restaurants nearby."

"We already bought food today."

"Yeah, but we're under our twenty-dollar budget."

"*Your* twenty-dollar budget."

"You're splitting hairs."

"We're only six dollars under."

"I'll buy us supper. Something simple. I promise."

"No," Blossom said firmly. "It's a slippery slope. It starts with something simple, and then we're dining on lobster tails, with white linen, candles and a bottle of wine that costs more than I make in a year."

"One can only hope," he said, and then, "I didn't realize that was such a hardship for you."

She didn't know how to explain to him that it was not that it was a hardship to be wined and dined and treated like a princess. But in the last little while, she'd become very aware that all of that got in the way of *this*.

An intense kind of togetherness.

"Can we just try it my way?" she asked.

"If we must," he said, pretending to grouse, but looking pretty indulgent.

"You know what? When you were pulling the boogie boards out of the shed, I think I saw a little barbecue in there."

"I love it," he said. "Barbecued steaks on the beach. Maybe lobster?"

"We're having steaks, all right," she promised him. "But with a twist. My way."

They found the barbecue and some propane, packed it into the vehicle. She made him stop at a mom-and-pop grocery store she had seen earlier.

"No, you stay here," she said. "I'm surprising you."

She came out of the store a few minutes later, with a bag full of goodies and a thankful heart. For some reason, her credit card was still working.

"I don't think you got steaks in that store," he said, sending her a sideways look.

"Define steak."

He gave her a look. "Define steak? That's kind of like saying define dog. It just is."

"No, it isn't. There are lots of different kind of dogs."

This kind of discussion was new for them. Blossom was increasingly aware she'd always just gone along with him. She was finding she *liked* sparring. She *liked* expressing her own ideas. She *liked* not always acquiescing, not always being pleasing, not always being agreeable.

"You're going to love this beach," he said. Joe didn't seem to mind her sparring with him at all. "The locals call it the Sixty-Nine."

She would not give him the satisfaction of blushing. "They do not!"

"They do." He wagged his eyebrows at her.

"You have a dirty mind."

"No," he said, "*you* have a dirty mind. Look over there."

"I don't see anything."

He was turning off the highway.

"Look at the mile marker."

She burst out laughing. The mile marker they turned at read 69.

"The actual name of the beach is Waialea. It's only just a few minutes from Hapuna, but it's totally different."

They got out at the parking area. Joe carried the barbecue down and Blossom carried the grocery bag. She stopped as they arrived at the beach.

Given its close proximity to Hapuna, it might have been in a different world. The bay was sheltered, so the waves were gentle, not powerful and white-capped and frothy as they had been at Hapuna. A large rock rose out of the center of the bay. Huge trees lined the edges of the fine sand beach.

But what was most different was the energy. Hapuna generated the same kind of energy as the waves that landed there.

Waialea was quiet, but not just because there were fewer people. It offered calm, respite from activity, a place to rest.

"I think this may be the most beautiful beach I've ever seen," Blossom breathed. She glanced at Joe's face.

He was so happy to show this to her, like a gift.

He set up the barbecue and lit it while she emptied the bag.

"Where are the steaks?" he asked, coming over and peering over her shoulder. "Blossom! Those look suspiciously like hot dogs."

"Don't say it like that!"

"Like what?"

"Like a snob! When we were growing up, we called them tube steaks. They were a mainstay in our house."

"Kind of like peanut butter?"

Again, she took that opportunity to reveal something of herself. "Hot dogs were more of a treat than peanut butter. I still love them."

This, she realized, as they sat side by side munching their hot dogs as the sun went down, was exactly what they had missed.

They'd had a whirlwind romance. Joe had treated her to the best of everything. He had given her entry to a world she had only dreamed existed. She had been swept off her feet.

But except for that one time camping, and maybe the evening that they had found Bartholomew, it suddenly felt as if there had not been nearly enough of *this*.

Just simple moments. Ordinary, and yet beyond ordinary. A blanket in the sand. A charred hot dog. Low music playing on Joe's cell phone. The last rays of the day's sun on their faces. The mynah birds singing out the day.

All of it raised up, somehow, with togetherness. With connection. With banter. With stories exchanged.

The next few days were crammed with new things and discoveries. She saw huge turtles resting in the charcoal-colored sand of Punalu'u; she saw and smelled steam vents in Volcano National Park; she walked in Nahuku, a five-hundred-year-old lava tube. She saw Kilauea's lava lake filling the crater, Halema'uma'u.

Everything was so new and exciting. Everything vibrated with a light. Because Joe was at her side.

But her favorite moments remained the quiet ones, where nothing appeared to be happening and everything that was life hummed just below the surface of that nothingness.

They spent every evening now at Waialea. They made it *their* thing to take dinner to the beach and watch the sun go down.

They watched children reluctant to get out of the water as their mothers packed up their things, they watched locals come down for an evening swim, they watched young men tossing a Frisbee as the day died behind them, they watched young couples stroll the beach, hand in hand.

It felt to Blossom as if everything was deepening between her and Joe, intensifying, just as the sunset deepened and intensified everything around it for that brief moment in time.

That intensity was in the way they enjoyed each other. In how the conversations were so easy. But that intensity also lived in the deep and comfortable silences. It was in the laughter they shared. It was in Blossom recognizing Joe had so many strengths completely unrelated to the fact he was wealthy.

Her sense of coming into herself just continued to deepen.

Whereas she had always held a part of herself back from Joe, always been *on* in some way, trying to win him, trying to be what Bliss had created instead of who and what she really was, now she felt herself relaxing.

Revealing who she really was.

She realized she had done them both a disservice by thinking she was not equal to him, that somehow she had to be forever grateful that a man like him could ever see anything in a girl like her.

She had brought those insecurities to the table, not him.

So, now they ate hot dogs—food of her childhood—at the beach. They were in the water so often she stopped wearing makeup altogether.

She lovingly wore one of her ten-dollar dresses every day, while the other dried from being washed in her bathroom sink the night before.

Joe seemed more relaxed, too.

He put his phone away. He didn't take calls or answer emails. He didn't seem quite so driven—as if he was managing to squeeze time together into his busy schedule.

"You know who was happy about the wedding being canceled?" she asked him one evening as they sat in the splendor of the setting sun in what had become their favorite place on Waialea.

He sighed. He looked at his watch. "We have four more days before we need to talk about the past. But don't say it was me who was happy about it, because it wasn't."

She could see how wise it was to have postponed this discussion. Because as soon as he said that, the hurt part of her wanted to say, *Why didn't you fight harder, then?*

Instead, Blossom said, "I wasn't going to say you."

"Who, then?" he asked with genuine surprise.

So, he didn't know his father had his doubts about her.

But it wasn't his father who came to mind.

"My mom," she said.

"That's not possible," Joe scoffed. "Sahara loves me."

"Her real name is Sheila."

"Your mom has a real name?"

"Yes, the only person you will ever meet with an 'also known as' who does not have a criminal record. Or at least not one I know of."

Again, there was a sense of stripping away the pretense around her family.

This is who we really are. What do you think?

"She gave herself a name that she thought suited her better."

"Interesting. It doesn't really suit her at all.

I mean it's exotic sounding, but the Sahara is a desert, and your mom is lively and full of life."

"She is that," Blossom said. "Some people would say kooky."

"Kooky in a cookie-cutter world. I've always loved that about her."

It felt as if he had passed a test Blossom was not aware she was giving. He *liked* her mom, kookiness and all.

"Well, my kooky mother was happy the wedding was called off, not because of you. She adores you. Which should give any sane person pause."

He laughed.

"Maybe *happy* is the wrong word, but there's nothing my mom loves more than an unexpected change of plans."

"That's pretty much the opposite of you."

"Mom didn't like the wedding. She looked at everything about it with increasing horror. I thought she'd be over the moon with excitement, overjoyed for me, but nope. The wedding plans seemed to cause her hand-wringing moments of aggravation.

"She actually hasn't ever expressed approval for any of the Blossoms and Bliss weddings, so far, even though she'll offer up her artistic skills in a pinch."

"Your mom isn't proud of you?" he asked with such genuine indignation Blossom wanted to kiss him. "That's just wrong. What is she thinking?"

"She thinks it's all too extravagant. She likes to remind us we weren't raised that way."

In fact, their mother was so lost in her artsy world she had barely raised them at all.

"The truth is, Bliss and I raised each other," Blossom confided in Joe, "living in that *twin* world of shared thoughts and dreams. We read each other fairy tales, built castles out of blankets and became the princesses in our own made-up worlds."

The truth was she and Bliss had longed for every value their fiercely single mother had eschewed: stability, family, home, romance and glamour.

Blossom had found them all with Joe.

She had almost become Mrs. Blackwell.

Before she had thrown it all away.

And yet, now it felt as though she were getting a second chance, and this time she was being given an opportunity to build a foundation based in honesty.

In who she authentically was.

But could Joe still possibly love her?

Over the last few days, it felt as if he could. The future was shimmering with possibility again.

She was endlessly trying to quell that part of her, but it felt like a bird beating its wings against a cage, wanting out, wanting to be free.

That part of her was hope. She could feel herself, ever so tentatively, opening the cage door.

And despite so much evidence in her life of how wrong things could go, it felt as if setting hope free made her braver than she had ever been.

"You know what?" Joe said as they finished another sunset supper at Waialea and packed away the remains of cold cuts and buns. "We need to book that night snorkel with manta rays if we're going to make that happen before we go."

Before we go.

That reminder that their time together in paradise was nearly done.

Of all the vouchers they had been given, that one made Blossom the most nervous. Getting in the ocean at night to swim with gigantic rays?

Any sensible person would say no.

But the brave person said yes.

He picked up his phone, which had been playing music, and looked up the excursion. "It's done," he said, pressing a button. "Tomorrow night. No going back now."

No going back now.

His phone returned to playing music. Recognition tickled along her spine.

"That just randomly appeared?" she asked him.

"It did."

It was a sign, she thought. *Their song.*

He pushed the volume button and the haunting opening notes of "Hunger" filled the air. The beach was nearly dark now and had emptied out. But it wouldn't have mattered if they were in a stadium with twenty thousand people looking on, she still would have said *yes* when he asked her to dance.

The distinctive voice of KaJee, the singer, swept across the beach and through her heart.

One of Joe's hands found its way to hers, and the other found the small of her back. Blossom felt the very same way she had felt when he had asked her to dance at the Lee wedding all those months ago.

As if she had been sleeping, and he would show her what it was to be awake.

As if she had been thirsty, and he would help her find her way to water and a long, cool drink.

As if she had been hungry, and he alone knew the way to a banquet hall rich with the kind of delights she had never even imagined.

They danced slowly, sinking into sand that still held the warmth of the day in their bare feet. They swayed together as if they were the only two people in the world.

They danced as if nothing had ever gone wrong between them.

They danced lost in the sensations of their closeness, the look in each other's eyes.

Blossom was aware, even as her focus on Joe was intense, she was hearing the song in a different way.

It was a musically complex song that required KaJee to use his complete range of vocals. The lyrics were unabashedly sexual. It was a song about need. About passion. About longing. About the fire that could ignite unexpectedly between two people.

But for the first time, Blossom was aware the song was unfolding on several different levels at once.

It seemed it was about physical intimacy, but dancing with Joe on the beach, she heard another layer.

The song was about a longing for connection, not just a physical one, but also a soul connection.

Maybe she was hearing it in a different way because she was a different person than she had been just a short few days ago.

He held her long after the last notes of the song faded, until the only sound on the beach was the sound of the waves and their breathing.

And then he dropped his mouth over hers and kissed her. Maybe because she was such a different person than she had been, it felt like it was the first time his lips were claiming hers.

It was exhilarating, and also the most natural thing in the world.

It felt physical, but the other connection was there, too.

It was literally breathtaking, as if he was taking the breath from her mouth. As she melted into him, Blossom had the sensation of melting into everything.

She and Joe and the world—sand beneath their feet, lapping waves, crying birds, the leathery whisper of the breeze in the palm fronds, the incredible light—all became one.

It was completely dark when he lifted his lips from hers. He traced them with his thumb and a sigh escaped him.

"Sorry," he said.

"Sorry?"

"Because I made a vow that we would see how it went for just a little while—a few days—without *this* changing everything, altering everything, becoming everything."

And then he stepped back from her, ran a hand through his hair and said, "It crowds out every other thing. That makes it so I can't think straight."

She wanted Joe with an ache so deep she did not feel as if she could survive without his touch, his lips, culmination.

"Joe," he said to himself, his tone wry, "you only had one mission. And you have failed."

He saw kissing her as a failure of his strength?

In this moment, love and hate warred within her. Because she actually hated him for having the discipline she did not possess.

He gathered up their things and headed off the beach. Back at Hale Alana, he said a crisp goodnight to her.

It wasn't until she was lying in bed that Blossom recognized her final disservice to Joe and to herself.

Because she had never been completely authentic with him, she had not recognized her power.

But she recognized it now. She chuckled to herself, and said out loud, "Oh, Joe, you are in for a very rough day tomorrow."

That particular force, what they had felt while they danced when their lips had met, did not want to be put back in the box.

And Blossom was suddenly as intent on letting it out as he was on keeping it in!

"What's on the agenda today?" she asked him the next morning, plunking herself down at the kitchen table. She was wearing only a T-shirt as she sipped her coffee. He wouldn't look at her.

"I thought we'd go up Mauna Kea. It's a dormant volcano and the world's largest astronomical observatory is up there."

That sounded perfectly dull. She saw Joe was retreating to the safety of being her Hawaiian tour guide.

She looked at him over the rim of her coffee cup. She stretched a leg and smiled to herself when she caught him sneaking a peek.

"You'll have to dress warmly," he said gruffly. "It can be really cold up there."

Aha! There was the Mauna Kea motivation! Keep them both dressed! But coming into her power gave Blossom the loveliest realization that she did not need to wear a bikini to be sexy.

And so she spent a delightful time tormenting him and teasing him, exploring what it meant to be a woman in ways she had not done before.

Flirting came naturally to other people.

Her sister had been born knowing how to use a glance, a provocative gnaw on her own lip, a hand on the hip, to send a message that she knew she had power and that she was not afraid to use it.

Blossom, for the first time in her life, was looking forward to practicing the age-old art of being a woman.

Letting out her new self—temptress!

It was cold at the visitor center—the first time Blossom had been cold since arriving in Hawaii. She used it as an excuse to tuck herself into Joe and wrap her arms around his waist.

Underneath his jacket, she could feel the hard beating of his heart.

"I know a way to warm up," she murmured, looking at his lips.

The look he returned to her was scorching. But then he moved away from her, determined, apparently to adhere to his no-touch rule.

"So do I!" And he broke away from her and did jumping jacks. It was really a measure of his desperation that the normally dignified Joe was doing jumping jacks!

"I was thinking more of the hot tub. When we get back to Hale Alana."

He frowned. He looked at his watch. "We won't have time," he decided. "Before the manta rays."

After that, Blossom took advantage of every opportunity to draw his attention to her lips, and her hips. Just like she didn't have to wear a bikini to be sexy, she realized *not* touching him was building the tension between them. She found that tension delightful.

She played word games, pretending innocence when some of what she said had double meanings.

She knew Joe had always adored her hair, and so she played with it unabashedly, running her hands through it, tossing it over her shoulder, gathering it up and twisting it into a rope that she stroked.

When they finally came down the mountain, he asked if she had packed a lunch.

"Not today. You can buy me lunch. There's supposed to be a really good restaurant in Waimea."

He mulled that over silently. "What about the money rule?" he asked.

"Rules are meant to be broken." She didn't have to say that meant she fully intended to break his rules, too.

"I know what you're up to," he said.

And the wind went out of her sails, a bit. Why

had he chosen the exact words his father had said to her?

The tiniest bit of doubt crept into her. Was she being manipulative to get what she wanted?

As it turned out, Joe made sure there was no time for the hot tub. After the Mauna Kea visit, they had a quick lunch—he didn't even offer to buy, so she had to hold her breath to see if her credit card would go through—and then he insisted on a tour of a coffee farm.

By the time they returned to Hale Alana they were pushing it to be on time for the manta ray swim.

Still, Joe was doing such a good job of resisting her that she decided it was time to haul out her teensiest bikini.

Joe actually looked smug when at the dock on Keauhou Bay, a crew member from the manta ray swim charter gave them both wetsuit shirts to zip on!

As he zipped his up it molded to him, from the broad sweep of his shoulders to the washboard perfection of his abs.

"It looks good on you," she told him throatily. How many days had they been together now, so much of it half-clad, as they went in and out of the ocean. She felt as if she could just never get enough of looking at him, and it felt wonderful to not be scared to let him know.

With a certain reluctance, he took her in.

"It looks good on you, too," he admitted, huskily.

It felt as if he had given a bit of ground.

She realized suddenly that she was really nervous. Because he'd given ground?

"I feel as if I can barely breathe," she confided in Joe.

But whether it was because of their upcoming swim with manta rays or because of that delicious tension between them—the silent scream for fulfillment—she was not sure.

He looked at her, deep into her eyes, for what felt like the first time today.

"Now you know how I've been feeling all day," he admitted.

CHAPTER FOURTEEN

"WHAT HAPPENED TO that woman who was afraid of sharks?"

Did Joe say that with a certain longing?

It was a legitimate question, Blossom thought. The truth was she did not feel anything like the woman who had arrived on Hawaii: defeated, hopeless, afraid.

She was now the antithesis of all those things. She had never embraced life as fully as she had over the last few days. And today, it felt as if she had entered a whole new level of boldness.

This was what she realized: the more she embraced life—the more she hoped—the more fearless she seemed to become.

And with that fearlessness came a sense of being alive.

That courage was flowing in her veins now. Here she was, Blossom DuPont, getting ready to go night snorkeling with manta rays.

Here she was, Blossom DuPont, sharing Hawaii with the man she—

"Mr. and Mrs. Blackwell?"

She started at being called that. Joe shot her a dark look that said, *Do not play with this.*

Of course, then she couldn't resist playing with it! Plus, it helped her with her nerves.

"That's us," she said, taking Joe's hand and leaning into him. "Newlyweds. This is our honeymoon, actually."

Joe broke away from her, shot her a warning look and stepped forward, his hand extended. "I'm Joe. This is Blossom."

Obviously wanting to avoid being called Mr. and Mrs. Blackwell again!

"I'm Gary, your captain tonight. I saw from the info card this private charter was a wedding gift. Are you enjoying your Hawaiian honeymoon?"

"Absolutely," Blossom said, and then mischievously, "What do you think, honey? Are you pleased with the honeymoon?"

He squinted at her. She should have taken that as a warning that she was playing a dangerous game.

But the new her seemed to enjoy flirting of all kinds, even with danger.

"The honeymoon has been completely unexpected," Joe said, watching her narrowly.

"Well, this is going to be the best part," Captain Gary told them, and then looked back and forth between them, embarrassed.

"Maybe not the *best* part," Joe said. "Right, *honey*?"

Blossom felt her cheeks catch fire. Well, she'd been playing with this all day. It was exciting that he was firing back.

She touched his arm, ran her fingers possessively over the muscle encased in that wet suit fabric. It was surprisingly erotic. "Right," she said.

Instead of backing away, he took her hand, kissed the fingertips, lingering. His gaze rested on her.

And there was no pretense in it. None at all.

He was warning her he was all done backing away. Blossom had been warned all her life about playing with fire. What no one ever told you was how completely exhilarating it was.

Captain Gary introduced them to the crew, went over a few safety rules and then they boarded the boat.

Captain Gary handed them snorkels.

"Oh, what do you know?" Joe said dryly, looking at his. "Real snorkels, not toys."

The sun set around them, absolutely stunning, as the boat headed out into ink-dark waters.

She shivered, and Joe, the perfect Mr. Blackwell, put his arm around her shoulder. It felt as if it belonged there. It felt, for a suspended moment, as if they really were Mr. and Mrs. Blackwell.

It didn't feel like a charade they were playing out for the captain and crew. It felt *real*. It was just one more perfect moment to add to her collection of perfect Hawaii moments.

And then what?

They had not once discussed what the future held.

And she was not, Blossom told herself with determination, going to ruin this moment by thinking of it now.

The boat cut its engine only a few minutes out of the bay. As always in the tropics, darkness had fallen with astonishing abruptness. The stars winked on above them. The lights of a hotel, sitting on a cliff not far away, twinkled in the water below it.

A crew member, Sara, went down a ladder and got into the water. Joe adjusted his snorkel and followed. Blossom hesitated on top of the ladder.

The water was as dark as ebony. For a moment, it felt as if her new boldness was going to flee her.

Who did she think she was? The *real* Blossom DuPont would never jump into a dark ocean at night. The *real* Blossom DuPont would never want to swim with fish that could weigh a thousand pounds or more!

A thousand pounds! Blossom thought. *That was—*

"Hey, Mrs. Blackwell! Jump," Joe called to her, the lights from the boat illuminating him against the darkness of the ocean.

His look was completely unguarded, and he

was looking at her as if he believed she could do anything. He held out his arms, and she pulled on the snorkel and went off the ladder. The water closed around her, and for a moment she felt primal terror.

But then Joe found her, and his arms closed around her, and through those crazy goggles, she could see the deep green of his eyes.

Blossom saw her real self reflected there. Her best self. She realized, astounded, she was in the ocean at night, about to swim with fish approximately the size of baby elephants, and she felt safe.

The lights on the boat turned off. Though the running lights remained on, the sensation of darkness was complete.

She, who had never felt truly safe in her whole life, felt safe in the black, shockingly cold waters of the ocean on a charcoal-dark night.

Because Joe's arms were around her. Because his eyes were taking her in so deeply, as if he could see straight to her soul. As if he saw the real her, and always had.

"So, nothing to it," Sara, the crew member, said. "Just follow me."

Her voice actually startled Blossom, because she had felt so totally alone with Joe, as if this whole watery world was just him and her.

They swam together holding hands, as Sara guided them a few yards from the boat to where a large flotation device—probably eight feet long and two feet wide—awaited them.

"Just lie flat on the water and look down through your goggles," Sara said.

Joe was right about the snorkel. The quality of it was evident. Blossom was thankful she was now quite familiar with snorkeling, and that she wasn't just learning it at this very moment. She was thankful for Joe at her side, making every experience an experiment in boldness.

"Hold on to this rung around the board. I'm going to turn on the lights now. The lights illuminate the plankton, which the rays eat," Sara explained. "It's against the law for you to deliberately touch a ray, but don't be alarmed if they touch you. There's no stinger in their tail. They're very gentle and very sensitive. They can actually feel the vibration from the beat of your heart."

When Sara said that, Blossom became aware of the beat of her heart, and was also electrically aware of her shoulder touching Joe's through the fabric of the wetsuits.

Was she imagining things, or could she feel the beat of his heart, too?

Strong and steady like him, something you could rely on in an uncertain world. She could definitely feel faint warmth coming off him, which she was grateful for, because even with the wetsuit top, she could feel how much colder the water felt at night.

Sara turned the lights on the board, and suddenly the inky ocean was illuminated below them. Joe let go of the board for a moment and gave Blossom a thumbs-up below the surface of the water, before grasping the rung again.

There was an incredible amount of plankton in the water, invisible to the eye during the day. Now Blossom could see hundreds of thousands of tiny dots floating upward, illuminated by the light. It felt as if they had been dropped inside a giant snow globe.

To her grave disappointment, nothing happened.

But then, Joe nudged her shoulder with his own, released one hand and pointed to the dark depths below them. Holding her breath, she looked where he indicated and spied a shadow emerging just out of range of the lights.

Suddenly she didn't know if the thrumming through her veins was excitement or terror. She was so glad Joe was beside her, a solid presence.

The shadow took form as it moved into the orb of light. It was a manta ray, and it was absolutely huge.

It came straight up toward them. Blossom could not believe the size of what she was seeing! Knowing something weighed a thousand pounds, or more, and actually seeing that—sharing the water with that—were two entirely different things!

The old Blossom might have panicked. But the

new Blossom drew in a deep breath through her snorkel, let go of the board for a minute, found Joe's hand and squeezed.

The ray, diamond-shaped, was easily twelve feet long, and its winglike fins were even larger. As it effortlessly closed the distance between them, its huge mouth was open, so they could see inside it to the marvel of its gills as it scooped up plankton.

A sense filled Blossom like nothing she had ever quite felt before.

To be this close to this magnificent creature of the sea left her feeling raw and awed.

The manta ray surged up in an impossibly graceful motion, until it was mere inches from Blossom and Joe. When it seemed it would collide with the board, or them, it arced leisurely backward, turned its large, spotted white belly up to the board, performed a slow-motion somersault that completed the circle that took it back into the depths, where it once again became invisible.

But then another manta ray, even larger than the first, appeared, soaring toward them. Up, up, up, belly turn, and back down.

And after that one, two manta rays came up together in an amazing ballet, white bellies nearly touching and then gently parting in opposite directions, each move perfectly choreographed, perfectly synchronized.

Another pair came from the bottom, rising toward Blossom and Joe. This time, as they came by her and Joe, Blossom felt the nudge of one of the huge fish.

That brief bump felt like a blessing.

Ray after ray after ray came, performing an impossibly delicate dance for creatures so gigantic. They were completely soundless. Sometimes they came as singles and sometimes in pairs. They would come out of the darkness, far, far below the board, rise to the light, parting, complete the circle and come again.

The cold seeped into her. Blossom had never had an experience like this. She was incredibly cold and her hands stretched out over her head holding the board ached unbearably. And yet she was nearly delirious with joy at the same time.

She had a sense of being extraordinarily privileged to witness these gentle giants doing their ancient dance.

Finally, Sara switched off the light. Blossom's limbs were so cold they felt heavy. Joe had to push her from behind to get her up the ladder and back onto the boat. Blossom was shaking uncontrollably. The wetsuit shirt must have offered some protection, but even with it she was cold to her core.

Joe was right behind her. Oblivious to his own discomfort, he helped her peel off the wetsuit shirt.

"I'm as frozen as I've ever been," she said

through chattering teeth, "and I'm Canadian! We're supposed to be used to the cold."

"I should have asked them to get us in sooner," Joe said regretfully. He toweled her hair tenderly, then wrapped the towel around her and rubbed hard. He looked around, found his hoodie and dropped it over her head.

"No," she said, still shivering. "I wouldn't have wanted it to end sooner. I've never felt that way before—so cold I was thinking, *please be over*, and so enthralled I was thinking, *please never end*, at the same time. It was the best thing I've ever experienced, ever." She paused, looked at him deeply. "Second best."

"That was so awesome," Sara said. "I've never, in all the time I've been doing this, had so many manta rays show up so continuously."

She beamed at Blossom and Joe. "Remember I said they can feel your heartbeats? You two must have incredible energy. Love is in the air!"

Blossom shot Joe a look to see his reaction to that.

He still had his wetsuit shirt on. He didn't react at all, focused on a hot mug of tea the captain had waiting. He passed it to Blossom.

He made sure she was looked after before he looked after himself. Only after she was sipping her tea did he peel off his own wetsuit.

And that was love, wasn't it? This simple, selfless force that showed itself in the most mundane things.

Passing your beloved a cup of tea.

Beloved.

Looking at him, his skin pebbled, his hair dripping water down his skin, Blossom was filled with a sense of knowing as she mulled over that word.

Beloved.

A truth, startling and ancient, rose up out of the darkness toward the light, just as those manta rays had.

The manta rays who *knew.*

Who could tell from the beat of your heart.

Of course, Blossom realized, she had always known. From the moment she had first met Joe, from the moment his hand had closed around hers and they had danced to "Hunger," her eyes looking into his, she had known.

Meant to be.

That feeling of knowing him had only grown as the months of their courtship went by, when she had said an exuberant yes to Joe's proposal.

She loved this man. She had never stopped and she would never stop. She didn't love him because he had money and could make her feel safe and secure forever.

She loved him because he was a man who would get down in the gutter to rescue a cat. She loved him because he was rock-steady, innately stable, in a world that could be anything but.

It wasn't Hawaii that was making her feel more alive, more bold, on fire with curiosity and a sense of discovery, though of course Hawaii was the most amazing backdrop for what she was experiencing.

Love.

Love made more exquisite by the fact it had nearly been lost.

Even with the roof up on the four-wheel drive vehicle, it seemed it was not made to hold the warmth that blasted out of the heater. She was still wearing Joe's hoodie, but her bathing suit was clammy against her skin, and she could not get warm on the way home. Her teeth continued to chatter. From the cold? From the enormity of what was singing inside her?

Or from some combination of both?

I love him. I love him. I love him.

And so, when they arrived at Hale Alana, it seemed like the most natural thing in the world when he came around to her side of the vehicle and lifted her out. Her arms twined around his neck as he scooped her up, with easy strength, into his arms.

She snuggled into his warmth. How could he be so warm?

On fire, almost.

He walked to the front door, juggled her weight easily, put in the code and carried her across the threshold.

She drew in her breath.

This was how it was supposed to have been. This was how it would have been if they had arrived here on their honeymoon.

What kind of miracle was it that time had rewound, and that they were being given a chance to do it right? To do it the way it had been meant to be all along?

Blossom reached up with her hand and explored the beautiful, familiar lines of Joe's face. For a moment, he looked as if he intended to resist her. But perhaps the cold had sapped some of his strength, too, because when she touched his lip with her finger, ever so gently, he growled, a low sound of surrender, deep in his throat.

Possibly the most beautiful sound Blossom had ever heard.

And then he nipped her finger, where it rested on his lip.

"Joe," she said, her voice hoarse with need, "I want you."

He drank her in, closed his eyes, and when he opened them again, a new light shone in them.

He went right through the house, slid open one of the back doors and carried her through it. With his elbow he turned on the pool lights and carried her across the stone deck to the hot tub. Only there did he set her down.

He had avoided this temptation once today. But

things that were meant to be could be avoided, but not stopped.

Her focus felt oddly wide—taking in the lush greenery around them, the delicate bloom of a hibiscus, the blue of the water, the steam rising off the hot tub—and narrow at the same time. As if Joe—that look in his eyes, the cut of his jaw, the line of his lips, the sea scent of him—was all there was in the entire world.

They drank each other in, in complete wonder, as if this was the very first time. He touched her hair with his hands. Reverent.

She slid into him, pressed herself against the full length of him, felt the sinewy strength of his muscles, the sensual, velvety softness of his skin.

Her flesh still felt as cold as marble, but his heat seeped into her, and she felt like a cold vessel slowly filling with warm fluid.

"Blossom," he said hoarsely, "are you—"

She answered him by claiming his lips with her own.

She knew what his question was going to be. Are you sure?

She had never been more sure of anything in her entire life. She took his lips with everything that Hawaii, that this time together, had given her.

"Aloha, Joe," she whispered. She took his lips with boldness and curiosity and welcome. And with absolute certainty.

He reached down to the hem of his hoodie and

tugged it over her head. She held her arms up willingly, to make it easier for him.

And then she stood before him in nothing but her bathing suit.

He reached behind her and, with a flick of his strong wrist, freed the top. It felt so good to be free of the cold, wet fabric, the tropical air touching her skin as if it was anointing it. She reached down and scraped the clingy wet bottom of the bathing suit down and then shinnied out of it.

And then she stood before him in nothing at all.

Eve before Adam, in their own private garden of Eden, at the dawn of time.

He shucked off his shorts and she shivered, but not from cold. Not this time. But from the raw, male beauty of him. And the recognition that it belonged to her.

Joe went into the hot tub and sat on the ledge that circled the interior of it. When she entered, he pulled her onto his lap, closing his arms around her.

His lips met hers, gently at first, inquisitive, welcoming.

"I've missed you so much," he murmured. "I thought we should try getting to know each other without this. I thought maybe it was making it so we didn't think clearly."

"And now?"

"I can't imagine knowing you without this. It's

not a capitulation to give in to this energy that is between us. It's a celebration. Of every single part of who we are, of every single part of you. It feels as if our very cells are singing to each other in recognition."

And then there were no more words. His lips were less gentle now. Demanding. Commanding.

And she willingly gave him everything he demanded. Everything he commanded.

Coming home to him.

Awakening to him. It was as if Hale Alana had always held the promise that was about to be realized between them.

CHAPTER FIFTEEN

WHEN IT FELT as if the water around them would boil from the heat they were generating, Joe once again scooped Blossom up into his arms. He strode through the darkened house and into his bedroom.

He laid her on the crisp, white lines of the bed and looked at her, his gaze dark with hunger. With passion. With a look of such complete wanting that any woman would die to see it on the face of her lover.

And then with a sigh of complete surrender, he laid himself on top of her. Holding his weight off her with his elbows, so that his skin skimmed hers, he took her in.

Tenderly with his eyes, and his lips, and his hands, he explored every inch of her. He started by flicking her lip with his tongue. And then each of her ears. He made his way slowly, exploring the curve of neck and collarbone, the swell of breast, the hollow of her belly button. He went from the top of her head to the tips of her toes, anointing her with fire.

And then, vibrating with exquisite and torturous tension, she turned the tables on him, scooted out from under him, pressed him into the deep softness of the bed.

She bent her head to explore every inch of him, reveling in his familiar lines, in the taste of him, in the feel of his silky skin beneath her tongue and her fingertips.

When they had teased and tantalized each other until their nerve endings were screaming with awareness and desire, they took it to the next level.

Somewhere, on this island, a volcano was erupting.

And they were, too, shooting fiery sparks up higher and higher, until the sparks seemed as if they would join the stars. But the sparks did not join the stars. They lost heat, cooled and fell back to the earth, where they dissolved.

Where they became hibiscus and manta ray, blue water, and black earth.

Where they became the beginning and the end.

Where they became nothing at all and everything there was.

Joe thought it was probably a good thing that he and Blossom had seen so much of the Big Island, and done so many things, before *this*.

Before they became lovers again.

Perhaps it was all that holding back that had

made their surrender after the night with manta rays so exquisite.

Now they were like people who had crawled across the desert to find the oasis, which was each other. They could not drink enough to quench the thirst. They were like starving people presented with a banquet. They could not leave the table.

There was no room for anything else, no inclination toward distractions. There was no more sightseeing, no more snorkeling, no more boogie boarding at Hapuna.

Hadn't he suspected this element—this intensity between them, this passion—clouded everything about their relationship?

Their last days in Hawaii they never left Hale Alana. They lounged around the pool with books, and they made love, and they had something to eat, and they made love, and they drank wine in the hot tub, and they made love,

And for something that clouded everything, Joe had never felt quite so clear.

He simply could not live without Blossom. He could not imagine a life without her in it. Tomorrow, they were leaving.

And still, neither of them had mentioned the future.

It was as if they had put the honeymoon before the horse!

It was time to address the future. To figure out

exactly where and why things had gone wrong, fix it and move on.

He was going to ask her to marry him. Again. It was obvious they were made to be together. He had the ring. Of course he had the ring! He'd kept it close to him since the day she'd given it back.

He found the bottle of champagne he had put in the fridge nine days ago.

"Hey," she said, coming into the kitchen. She was in bare feet and her hair was tousled. She was wearing a Hawaiian shirt that she had insisted on buying for him on one of their rare excursions, when hunger had forced them out of Hale Alana.

She was wearing nothing besides that shirt.

"I thought we weren't spending any money," he'd said when she had given it to him as a gift.

"No, you aren't spending any money. I can spend until my credit card is declined. Which I'm amazed hasn't happened already."

There was a new openness about her. The Blossom he'd been engaged to before would have never been so open about her financial difficulties. Not that she really had any financial difficulties. Bliss had texted him that it was all looked after.

He'd let her know tonight.

The shirt was neon green, covered in pink flowers.

It was the kind of thing he never wore. But he had worn it for her. Because it made her laugh.

"That shirt looks way better on you," he said.

"Thanks," she said, and gave him a smile that almost made him forget he was a man on a mission. "Those are my favorite shorts on you, too."

He glanced down at himself. Of course it was the pelican shorts. The ring felt as if it was burning a hole in his pocket.

"What's the occasion?" she said, nodding at the champagne.

"Our last night here," he said. "I thought we should celebrate."

"Oh." Her face fell, as if she thought he wanted to celebrate the fact it was their last night. This was exactly what had gotten them in trouble last time.

She was so sensitive. She was always looking for trouble.

Her sister had said she didn't believe good things could happen to her.

He frowned down at the champagne bottle. Would she think he was a good thing? He'd thought so last time.

But how quickly she had run away from it all.

He remembered the first time he'd proposed. He'd rented a penthouse suite at the best hotel in Vancouver. He'd filled up the room with roses and scattered rose petals on the bed. He'd had a private dinner catered for them.

And then, he'd gotten down on one knee.

"Do you feel like some popcorn?" she asked, interrupting Joe's memories of the last proposal.

"Sure."

In what world did popcorn go with champagne and wedding proposals?

His world. His world with her in it. *Their world.*

"You can thank me that the cork didn't pop," he said, sliding it from the bottle.

"Isn't it supposed to pop? And the champagne go all over the place?"

"That's what happens if you don't chill the bottle. The champagne is too gassy if you try to open it warm. And if you serve it too cold, it loses some of its flavor."

"Rich people stuff," she said. And then she gave him a wink, came and took the bottle from him and took a drink straight from it She passed it back to him. "I wouldn't want you to become a snob," she said.

Joe took a drink straight from the bottle, too. Why not just go with it? It's not as if the formal proposal that he had so carefully orchestrated all those months ago had ended well.

A few minutes later, they sat in an egg-shaped, pillow-stuffed chair for two, at the pool. They watched the stars come out, took turns sipping from the bottle of champagne, and munched popcorn.

"You want to go for a swim?" Blossom asked him, her voice husky.

He knew what that meant. She'd shuck off that

shirt and swim in the pool nude, an enchantress who could not be resisted.

There *it* was, getting in the way, the ultimate distraction, that hum of electricity and awareness between them. Why did she make such a mockery of all his missions?

But he was determined it wasn't going to foil his plans tonight.

"Maybe later. Right now, I want to ask you—"

To marry me.

He hesitated. Maybe they *should* go for a swim. He was sweating, and it wasn't because of the gentle warmth of the evening, either.

"I figured we'd talk about *that* tonight," she said.

"What?" Had she guessed? He was trying to feel around in his pocket for the ring, without her noticing.

"That day in Essence that I gave you back the ring."

He didn't want to talk about that, at all. He wanted to be the one to give her back the ring this time. Under better circumstances, of course.

"It's just that all of a sudden," she said softly, "you seemed reluctant about the wedding. About me."

"I wasn't ever reluctant about you, Blossom, ever."

And he was about to prove it, if she'd just let him.

"I was feeling insecure anyway, because of something that had happened."

His fingers closed around the ring in his pocket.

"Remember when we had dinner at your parents'? It was the Sunday before we met for lunch."

"Barely," he said.

He should definitely get down on one knee.

"I probably wouldn't remember it, either, except something happened."

"Something happened," he repeated absently. "At my parents' house?"

In his mind he rehearsed, *Blossom, I'm crazy about you. I can't imagine life without—*

"Your dad was waiting for me when I came out of the bathroom. He said something to me."

His proposal rehearsal came to an abrupt end inside his own head. Joe felt dread crawling along his spine. "What did he say?"

"He said, *'I know what you're up to.'*"

Joe thought he should have known as soon as the champagne didn't go quite as planned, that maybe this proposal was going to go sideways.

"As if I was sneaking my way into the Blackwell family, and he could see right through me."

Joe drew in a sharp breath. "Why didn't you tell me?"

"I was shocked. And embarrassed. I wondered if I had heard him right."

He drew in a deep breath. It was time to tell her. Long past time, really.

"I think you heard him right," Joe said slowly. "I wish I'd known he said that to you. That's why I was putting out feelers about maybe changing the wedding. My mom had just told me they couldn't come. Wouldn't."

"To our wedding?"

He heard the distress in her voice. "Not because of you, Blossom. They adore you."

"Well, apparently not your dad," she said. "Your parents had decided not to come to our wedding? And you didn't tell me?"

"Blossom," he said more sharply than he intended. "It's not about you!"

"Why should it be different now? Both you and Bliss have let me know it was all about me ever since I started planning the wedding."

What was it about the damned wedding that got her going like this? He took his fingers off the ring. In fact, he took his hand out of his pocket.

"My dad's sick," he told her.

She blinked. The agitation fled her face. "What? What's wrong?"

"They're not exactly sure," Joe admitted. "There hasn't been an official diagnosis. But there are suspicions. My mom's been noticing he was *off* for quite a while. I mean, as soon as she told me, I could think of things, too. Odd things. Just like what you just mentioned. Hostility. An accusatory tone when it's not called for."

"Joe! What do they think it is?"

The words felt so painful. Did saying them make the thing he most wanted not to be real, real? Was that why he'd avoided telling her?

"His doctor thinks it's a form of dementia."

There. He'd said it out loud.

"Not the most typical form," he continued, realizing it felt good to talk about it, as if he'd been keeping a dirty secret. "Because his working memory is pretty good. Mom said they think it's a behavioral variant. So, a complete lack of filters. Inappropriate behavior. Outbursts."

"Joe, I'm so sorry," she said. "I don't understand why you didn't just tell me."

I didn't want it to be real.

"I had just heard," he said. "Minutes before I met you. Mom asked me not to tell anyone. Not just yet. She's trying to protect him. She thinks people will look at him differently once they know."

Blossom stared at him. "And I'm *anyone?*"

Joe didn't like that look on her face.

"Not trying to make it all about me," Blossom said, and there was no mistaking the edge to her voice, "but you and I were two weeks from getting married. I was two weeks away from being part of your family.

"Actually, want to hear something funny? I already thought of myself as part of your family. But I guess not. I couldn't be trusted with devastating family news. I couldn't be trusted to do the right thing. I was placed on the outside of the circle."

"That's not it." The relief he had felt confiding in her was fleeing. Fast.

"Joe, I would have changed our wedding plans in a heartbeat if I'd known any of this. You didn't have to start hinting about camping instead. One line from you, the truth, and all of this could have been avoided."

All of this could have been avoided?

Did she mean the last ten days? Okay, it hadn't been the honeymoon as planned.

He thought of snorkeling, and boogie boarding. He thought of lava forming a lake in a volcano, and the cool, dark depths of a lava tube.

He thought of wonder and laughter. In some ways it had been so much better than anything they could have ever planned. She regretted the last days, when they had been the best in his life?

"What if I have it?" he asked, aware, somehow, that was the real question, the real concern.

She stared at him. Tears sparked in her eyes. Already pitying him, just as he'd feared.

"You know what's sad?" she asked him tersely, no pity in her voice at all. "You think you're protecting me from the potential for something horrible happening in the future."

That was it exactly. So, why didn't she look pleased?

"But it's really about not trusting me. To be

strong enough. To know the right things to do. To be there unfailingly through life's challenges. To trust love will give us what we need to live up to every single vow we would have taken if we had gone through with the wedding."

He was stunned by that perspective.

"Is there anything else you're keeping from me?" she said snootily.

How dare she treat him as if he was allergic to the truth because of one omission? But then he realized there was something else he *was* keeping from her.

"The reason your credit card hasn't been declined is because I paid for the wedding," he said.

She looked aghast, as if he had announced that he was involved in the illegal trade of drugs.

"I asked you not to!" she stormed.

"It's not a big deal."

"It's not a big deal *to you*. It's a big deal to me. It's about respect."

"You know what it's really about?" he asked her. "You're just spoiling for a fight. Because your life has been too good, and it's just like Bliss said. You cannot believe good things can happen to you."

"Bliss and you discussed me?"

"Not exactly," he said uncomfortably. "And don't act as if Bliss and you haven't discussed me."

"That is not the same thing, at all."

"And, Miss High and Mighty, while we're at it, don't act as if you trusted me with any of your family secrets, either."

"Miss High and Mighty?" she said.

"Yeah, and thank God it isn't Mrs." He was glad that ring was still in his pocket, because if he'd given it to her, he was pretty sure she would have thrown it back at him right about now.

The Mrs. crack hit. He wished as soon as it had left his mouth he could take it back.

She tossed her hair over her shoulder. Picked up her towel and stomped away. He could hear her crashing around in her bedroom.

And then the front door opened and slammed shut.

He heard the vehicle start. She was stealing his car. For a moment he felt worried. He should go after her, but how? He didn't have a vehicle.

Then he thought wearily, *let her go*.

Blossom barely drove out of the driveway. She hadn't had enough to drink that she needed to worry about that—only three or four sips of champagne—but she was shaking with emotion.

She found some shrubs and pulled over, turned off the vehicle. Her plane wasn't scheduled to leave until tomorrow. But thank goodness she still *had* a plane scheduled to leave tomorrow, even though they had planned to return to Vancouver on Joe's private jet.

Plans.

Her mother was fond of saying that was what you made if you wanted to make the gods laugh.

Blossom had allowed herself to get her hopes up one more time.

Didn't she ever learn?

CHAPTER SIXTEEN

IT WAS JUST exactly what Joe had thrown in her face, Blossom reflected. She could not believe good things could happen to her. And there was a good reason for that. Because they didn't!

It was a shock about his dad. She suddenly felt ashamed of herself. She *had* made it all about *her*. This news must be devastating for Joe.

On the other hand, he'd played it awfully close to his chest. She could understand at the restaurant the day she had cancelled the wedding, that Joe had just heard the news about his father, that he hadn't known what to do with it. But now? He'd had plenty of opportunities over the last days to tell her what was going on.

But, no, he had chosen not to trust her with it.

And Joe had said his dad's illness removed his filters. So did that mean James now said what he really thought all along, instead of hiding it? Did Mr. Blackwell now blurt out whatever was on his mind, unable to stop it with manners and decorum?

She had more immediate problems than what Joe's dad really thought of her. What was she going to do for tonight?

Her credit card was paid off. She could go get a hotel room.

But thinking about that credit card being paid off filled her with a fresh wave of fury. How dare Joe? She was going to have to pay him back. It was a point of pride now. So, she couldn't be wasting any money on a hotel room.

She crawled into the back seat.

"It's not as if living in a car is anything new to you," she told herself.

And at least she didn't have to worry about being cold.

That was the last time, for a long while, that Blossom didn't have to worry about cold. Back in Vancouver, the promise of that bright spring day when she had sashayed through Gastown to meet Joe at Essence had fizzled.

It was raining in the coastal city as if it never planned to stop. Cold winds drove the constant drizzle off the ocean. The skies were leaden and gray. The spring flowers were drooping and turned in on themselves. In contrast to Hawaii, it was all exceedingly depressing.

Though, admittedly, the dreariness matched her mood. For the first time in her memory, she and Bliss were standoffish with each other.

They weren't exactly fighting, though that might have been better.

No, they had argued about Joe paying for the wedding. Blossom had insisted they give him back his money, and Bliss had, maybe sensibly, refused.

"I'm not risking everything I—" *I, not we* "—have worked so hard for because you're making a point of pride. If you want to pay him back, you do that, but you save your own money to do it. It's not coming out of the company."

Blossom didn't address her sister's betrayal—talking about her with Joe behind her back. Instead, they lived in this state of strained aloofness at home and at work, which left Blossom feeling as alone as she had ever felt in her life.

Still, she had an obligation, ironically, to plan happily-ever-afters for others.

And oddly, she still loved the work, and immersed herself in it as completely as she could.

Finally, one night when she was in bed, her door creaked open and Bliss peeked in.

"I can't stand it anymore," Bliss said, her voice breaking.

"Me, either." Blossom scooted over in the bed. As Bliss lay down beside her, Bartholomew, Blossom's constant companion, gave an annoyed mew of protest at being replaced and hopped off the bed.

Blossom and Bliss both sighed.

"You're not just mad at me about the money, are you?" Bliss asked.

"I'm mad at the whole world," Blossom admitted. "I have not singled you out."

Bliss laughed. It was so good to hear her sister's laughter.

"I'm not as mad about the money as you talking to Joe behind my back," Blossom said. "You told him I didn't believe good things can happen to me."

"Yes, I did," Bliss said, not in the least contrite. "I also told him you're afraid to hope. I guess I thought I could help him fix things between you. But now I've realized I made an error. No matter how much he loves you, Joe can't fix that, Blossom. He can't fix your suspicion of happiness, your fear of hope. Only you can do that."

No matter how much he loves you.

Blossom felt the absolute truth of that. He loved her. And she had run away from it, not once but twice.

Both times, she had run away on the flimsiest of excuses.

Not because she didn't believe in his love.

But somehow, because she believed she was not worthy of it. Somehow, she believed it would hurt less to give up on it now than if it all fell apart later. When she had allowed herself to love him even more.

Wasn't that part of what had happened in Hawaii?

She was falling in love with him even more.

Leaving herself even more vulnerable to the pain of the inevitable.

"Things never worked out for us, Bliss. Every time we ever hoped for anything—whether it was a home that we could stay in, or a normal birthday party, or the promise of a fairy-tale senior prom—we never, ever got it."

Bliss was silent for a moment.

"We got something else instead," she finally said, quietly and firmly.

"What?" Blossom made no attempt to take the skeptical edge out of her voice.

"Creativity, resiliency, an ability to adapt quickly, to think on our feet when things don't go right. It's really why we're in this business."

"Creating the happily-ever-afters that we dreamed of and never got?"

"No, silly, believing in love. Don't you see? Whether we were living in a car or surviving the snubs of Mary-Beth—"

"It was Beth-Anne."

"Our love for each other got us through. I mean Mom was—is—flawed and wacky and eccentric and spontaneous. But have you ever once doubted she loved us?"

"No," Blossom said. "Not even once."

"That's why Blossoms and Bliss is such a success. Because that single message underlies every single thing we do. Because we've lived it, and so we know the absolute truth of it."

"And what is that message?" Blossom whispered.

"Love will get us through."

Try as he might to fill his days with activities, with business, with outings with Lance and his other pals, Joe could not stop thinking about Blossom. And Hawaii.

At least this time he wasn't trying to drown his sorrows. Somehow, he knew he needed absolute clarity.

And part of that clarity was that when he thought about Hawaii, it was not the many adventures—snorkeling, swimming with manta rays, exploring the mysteries of the volcano—that occupied his thoughts.

Nor was it the exquisite days after that night swim, where the chemistry between them had exploded and the world had become totally about their exquisite and joyous pleasure in each other.

Instead, Joe thought of the simplest of things, those quiet evenings at Waialea, just him and her, shoulders touching, the sun going down. Hot dogs. Spontaneous dancing. Talking. Connecting.

And he thought, often, of Blossom revealing her secrets to him.

Living in a car.

A jar of peanut butter making her feel safe.

That seventh birthday party with the ponies.

In those revelations was the secret to why she had run away from him, not just once, but twice.

Pride nursed his resentments and stoked his anger and his utter frustration with her. How could she be so unreasonable? Pride told him to let her go.

But love wouldn't let him.

Love insisted on revisiting Waialea, and remembering not so much what they had said and done, but how it had felt.

Love ached for the Blossom that didn't believe good things could happen to her—and then set out to make sure they didn't.

Love ached for the Blossom who was afraid to hope—and sabotaged all the things that could bring her happiness because of that.

Love told him that it required him to be a better man.

Love told him to ride in on his white charger and rescue her.

And in the act of rescuing her, somehow he would also rescue himself.

He realized the time for thinking—the endless loop it got him on—was over. The time was for action.

They could either have a life together or they couldn't, but he needed to satisfy that question in himself, once and for all.

No preparation this time. Just the ring in his

pocket and a quick stop at the grocery store, a walk through the chilling rain.

He stood outside Blossoms and Bliss.

This building, he realized, represented her deepest self. The part of her that wanted to believe in dreams.

He rang the doorbell.

It was Bliss who answered. Her eyes widened when she saw him, and then she stood up on her tiptoes and kissed his cheek in welcome, as if he was her long-lost brother returned home.

Which gave him great hope.

"I was just stepping out," she said, grabbing her raincoat off a hanger beside the door and slipping into the night.

Joe went up the stairs to the apartment above the storefront.

Blossom was curled up on one end of the couch, a blanket over her legs, her feet tucked underneath her, so engrossed in a television program she didn't look up.

Bartholomew was enjoying her lap and ear rubs and gave Joe the baleful look of one who recognizes a competitor for affection.

Thanks, buddy. Remember who saved your life?

Unless he was mistaken, Blossom was wearing one of his T-shirts. That gave him as much hope as Bliss' peck on the cheek.

"They eliminated Nathan and Kim," she said. "Who was at the door?"

And then she looked up.

And the look on her face deepened his hope again.

"Joe. Oh! W-what? W-why?"

He took off his wet coat, as if she'd invited him to. He went and sat beside her on the couch. Bartholomew gave him a dirty look, jumped down and stalked off.

"How's your dad?" she asked softly.

The question made him realize why he was here. It made him see who she really was.

"It's a new reality for all of us," he said, quietly. "I'm getting through it."

"Love does that," she said quietly. "Gets people through. The impossible. The heartbreaking."

"That's what I've learned from you, Blossom."

"From me?"

"When I look at the challenges you had growing up, I can see so clearly what you can't always see. They didn't make you less. They made you more. More strong. More compassionate. More creative. More resilient."

"Bliss just said that," she whispered.

"And now I see my dad's illness is the same thing. It has to make us more. Not less. It has to.

"And I'm not sure if I can live without you showing me the way, Blossom. Showing me the way to turn lead into gold, darkness into light, tests into triumphs."

"Me?" she squeaked.

"Yes, you," he said. "The one who never sees herself clearly. I promise you this—I will always see you, even when you lose sight of yourself. I will always see your innate courage. Your innate hopefulness. Your ability to dream. Always."

She went absolutely still, but tears were shining in her eyes.

"I brought you something," he said. He handed her the paper bag, gone soft from the rain.

She looked at him.

And he saw it.

Just a flicker of what she didn't want him to see. The naked love for him that was making her so vulnerable. And so, so afraid.

And then she opened the bag. She stared at the contents. Her face crumpled. The tears that had been shining in her eyes slid free. And then she began to weep, noisily.

Peanut butter. His simple message to her.

"I want you to know," he said, "things will be okay."

She came gently into his arms, trustingly, like that soaked kitten of all those months ago. Even though she was sobbing against him, it was homecoming.

He lifted her chin and scanned her tearstained face.

And he saw everything there that he needed to see. Hope and fear of hope. Happiness and fear of happiness.

But also that innate courage he loved so much, the courage of being willing to give life—and love—more chances.

He didn't ask her this time. He stated his truth. "I need to marry you."

"Oh, Joe, I've been so—"

"Scared?"

"Yes."

"I don't want you to be scared anymore. I want us to get married, and I want to spend every day showing you things will be okay. Every. Single. Day. And every single day you can show me what pure bravery looks like and where it leads. What do you say?"

She gave him a smile and hugged that jar of peanut butter to herself.

In that smile was everything that Blossom was: valiant and flawed. And totally, totally in love with him. Enough in love with him to grab on to that hope he held out to her.

Even with the rain pounding outside her window, the sun came out in his world.

"Yes," she whispered. And then louder, "I say yes."

Joe laid his forehead against hers.

"Aloha, Blossom."

CHAPTER SEVENTEEN

THE SUN WAS going down over Waialea Beach. As always, everything stopped in Hawaii as people paid homage, with their quiet reverence, to another day in paradise.

Blossom DuPont and Joe Blackwell said *I do* just before that moment when the whole world went still.

It was not the wedding Blossom had imagined. It was, indeed, not like any wedding that Blossoms and Bliss had ever planned.

On rare occasions, she thought, her hand in Joe's as she leaned into the shoulder of *her husband*, things went better than you could possibly ever plan them.

And their wedding was one of those occasions.

There was a tropical storm brewing over the Pacific, but it had held off. It was predicted to be bad enough that they had considered canceling, but in the end, they had decided to take their chances.

Things will be okay.

And they had been. As the day gave way to night, the weather could not have been more perfect.

She was barefoot, in the simplest of white dresses—Wally Wiggles, twenty-nine dollars and ninety-nine cents—with a lei of frangipani in her hair that fell loose over her shoulders.

Joe was barefoot and in a crisp white shirt, paired with the wildest shorts they could find, turquoise and black with flowers all over them.

Bliss stood beside her, and his best friend, Lance, stood beside him. The only little glitch seemed to be some tension between Lance and Bliss.

Her mom was there, and Joe's mom and dad. The three parents stood as a unit.

Indeed, Sahara had stepped up to the plate in unexpected ways when she had heard about James's illness. She had seen that Celia was completely overwhelmed by the new reality of her husband, and quietly, and with certainty, she was just there.

Offering a hand. Showing James how to paint a picture. Watching a movie with him. Allowing Celia time away.

Her mother, unexpectedly, maybe because of her artistic soul, found ways to connect to James. Often, you could hear them laughing together.

"That's what family does," Sahara had said, surprised when Joe expressed his gratitude for her being there, for her finding remnants of his father that seemed to be lost.

But Joe himself was also there for his father, and

watching his patience and strength in the face of such a devastating illness only made Blossom love this man, who was now her husband, more. On every level, Joe had shown how loyal he was, how able to be there when the going got tough, how family was already a vow—his deepest obligation— even if no words were spoken out loud.

Blossom glanced over at Joe's dad. He glared back at her.

"I know what you're up to," James yelled, as Celia and Sahara both tried to shush him.

Blossom gave her new husband's hand one last squeeze and went over to his father. She took James's hands and looked deeply into his eyes.

She looked at him with intuition. More and more, Blossom was aware of the gifts her mother had given her. And this was one of them.

Intuition. Seeing with your soul, instead of your thoughts.

Having the odd period when peanut butter was your mainstay seemed like a small price to pay for such an incredible gift.

As she looked at James, Blossom saw Joe there, in his father's eyes. She saw who Mr. Blackwell really was beneath this crushing illness. She saw the strength in him, the calm, the intelligence.

"I love you," she said to him quietly, from the bottom of her heart, this man who had been part of that incredible family unit that had made Joe everything he was.

James went very still. The angry look left his face. His eyes teared up.

Wasn't that just what everyone wanted, after all? To be seen?

She kissed both his cheeks, let go of his hands and hugged her mother-in-law.

She found herself in her mother's arms. Sahara kissed the top of her head, held her away from her and smiled through tears. Her pride and her love shone in her eyes.

"Most beautiful bride ever," her mom said. "Best wedding *ever.*"

That was true. Because what made a wedding the best was being surrounded by the people you cared most deeply about. And these people here were the ones who had proved they would stand with them, no matter what.

What made a wedding the best was the love singing between her and Joe. Love that had been tested. Love that had walked through the fire and come out the other side, made stronger for the scorching, like wood that had been preserved with the Japanese burning technique *shou sugi ban*.

There was a picnic basket there, and now Joe took out a bottle of champagne, iced, so that the cork wouldn't pop, and Blossom handed out plastic glasses.

They toasted. The glory of the day. The sunset. Each other. And each member of the wedding party. Their families. And life. And the future.

Sahara, of course, had quite a lengthy speech she wanted to make, and as she made it, out of the corner of her eye, Blossom noticed Bliss slipping away. She set down her glass and went and followed her.

Bliss had found her way into the huge monkey pod trees that lined the upper area of Waialea. She looked gorgeous sitting there in the sand, looking out to sea in the fading light, her hair being lifted by the wind, like a girl in a painting.

She always had flair, and she had chosen a short, pink dress to stand beside her twin. Now her arms were wrapped around her naked knees, and her expression pensive.

The wind was coming up, seemingly out of nowhere, and Bliss shivered. Blossom came and sat down beside her, put her arm around her. In the distance, they could still see the wedding party.

"I'm just like a manta ray," she told Bliss. "I can feel the beating of your heart."

Bliss laid her head on her shoulder.

"Is something wrong?" Blossom asked her quietly.

"Of course not! Most perfect day ever!"

"You know, you can lie to other people, but not to me. Is something up between you and Lance? I sense a bit of tension."

"Oh, *him*," Bliss said, as if he were a bothersome fly. "No, that's not it."

"You can tell me."

Bliss slid her a look and then sighed. "You know, when you came here for your honeymoon that wasn't—and then was—it was the longest we'd ever been apart. I've never been without you in my life before. The constant. My family. I have no doubt of Mom's love for us—and I adore the kind of over-the-top extravagance of it—but constant she was not."

Blossom got exactly what Bliss was saying.

"I guess I'm scared, Blossom," her twin confided in her. "That everything between us will change now that you're married. That I won't be the most important person in your life anymore. And then, when you have kids…" Her voice drifted away.

Blossom tightened her hold around her sister's slender shoulders.

"Love isn't like that," Blossom said finally, measuring her words. "I don't have less of it to give you because I'm in love with Joe. It multiplies. It doesn't divide. I have more of it than ever."

"Love works in mysterious ways," Bliss said with a sigh. "According to Ed Sheeran."

Did her gaze drift to Lance for just a second when she said that?

"Who is that?"

"A singer. We play him at every wedding."

"That's why you're in charge of music."

"You're such a dork sometimes, Blossom."

"A dork is actually a whale's penis."

"The fact that you know that proves my point exactly."

"Just for the record," Blossom said, "I already know you'll be the best auntie ever."

"That's true," Bliss said, some of her old self back in the grin she gave Blossom. "I will be really good at that. Evil, though. The one slipping the kids chocolate before dinner and bringing them to movies they're not allowed to see."

The silence stretched between them, comfortable.

"How come you've never gotten married, Bliss?" Blossom asked. She could see her sister as a mom. The fun element aside, Bliss had so much love to give. "I mean you've had about a million men fall in love with you."

"Not that many. Nine hundred thousand."

They both chuckled.

"There's the rub," Bliss said thoughtfully. "I've had all those men fall in love with me, and I've never fallen in love back."

"Not even once?"

"No."

"Do you want to?"

"Yes."

The silence was long, again, and then Bliss said, "I'm scared now, though. I've broken so many hearts that when I fall in love, he's going to break mine. I just know it. Lance is the kind of guy who could show me what a bitch karma can be."

Blossom didn't say anything.

"He asked me out after the Lee wedding."

"He did?"

"You were so wrapped up in Joe you didn't notice him hanging around when we were cleaning up. What a jerk! He'd come with someone else. That's why when he said he'd like to see me, I said no. He's actually miffed about it. I don't think he's had women say no to him very often."

Blossom thought of Joe's tall, dark and handsome friend. She was pretty sure Bliss was right on that account.

"Anyway, he persisted. I threw a vase of flowers at him."

Blossom contemplated this overreaction with interest. It was not like Bliss. At all.

Blossom filed that away about Lance. "Karma," she said thoughtfully. "Now you sound like Mom."

"Sometimes I wonder if I'll turn into her." Bliss sighed pensively. "Flaky. Alone."

"You won't. I won't let you. You'll always have me."

"And you'll always have me," Bliss said. "Let's go back."

The sisters stood up together and walked back to the gathering on the beach, arm in arm.

Their mother was looking through the cooler. "What's in here?"

Joe saw Blossom coming. His expression was so tender, and so welcoming. He came toward her, and she slipped away from Bliss and toward him.

Toward every single thing she had ever hoped for her future.

He put his arms around her waist, looked deeply into her eyes and said, with the most wonderful smile tickling the beautiful line of his mouth, "You know what's in that cooler?"

"Peanut butter?" she heard her mother, the one who hated extravagance, exclaim, appalled. "Who serves peanut butter at a wedding?"

* * * * *

Look out for the next story in the
Blossom and Bliss Weddings duet
coming soon!

And if you enjoyed this story, check out these
other great reads from Cara Colter:

Snowed In with the Billionaire
Bahamas Escape with the Best Man
Snowbound with the Prince

All available now!